"There's not one solid piece of evidence to charge this man!"

"There's plenty," Mercer protested. "The girl's made up an incredible story to protect her father. What if we make a mistake? The press would be—"

Judith interrupted. "What the press does isn't relevant. This is a prosecutorial decision. It ought to be based on the facts of the case. *Only* the facts."

Mercer ignored her. "I say we charge him and we go forward with the case."

"I can't tell you how strongly I feel about this. Charging an innocent man? It's the most unethical thing I can think of." Something inside Judith snapped. Putting herself on the line, she couldn't stop herself. "I can't imagine working in an office that would do such a thing."

Silence followed as Judith turned and walked out the door.

Other Avon Books by
Patricia D. Benke

ABOVE THE LAW

CRUEL JUSTICE

PATRICIA D. BENKE

AVON BOOKS ◆ NEW YORK

AVON BOOKS, INC.
1350 Avenue of the Americas
New York, New York 10019

Copyright © 1999 by Patricia D. Benke
Back cover author photo by Kira Corsa
Published by arrangement with the author
Library of Congress Catalog Card Number: 98-94852
ISBN: 0-380-79016-5
www.avonbooks.com

First Avon Books Printing: July 1999

AVON TRADEMARK REG. U.S. PAT. OFF. AND IN OTHER COUNTRIES, MARCA REGISTRADA, HECHO EN U.S.A.

Printed in the U.S.A.

WCD   10 9 8 7 6 5 4 3 2 1

Prologue

———

JUDITH THORNTON LOOKED out over the four acres of green grass: at the children moving, crisscrossing the soccer fields; at the sudden crash of bodies and the referee in the black knit shirt with the white V-neck collar, standing over the two boys tangled on the ground. He paused, wrote something on a pad of paper, and raised his hand to the sky, a yellow card at his fingertips. She tried to remember. Yellow was a foul. It was red that got you ejected from the game. From the other side of the field several parents let loose a barrage of verbal assaults on the referee; from the home team coach came a polite but audible "Thank you, ref."

It was a different sport, soccer. No hitting from behind. No scissor kicks to the ankles. It was a plenty physical game, but you didn't hurt people— at least, not intentionally.

"Ref . . . sub," the coach yelled. The linesman raised his black and red checkered flag to draw the referee's attention to the request and a sweating, panting boy raced to the sideline as another took his place. The coach, an island of calm in a torrent of emotion, turned to the exhausted youth and put-

1

ting his arm solidly around his shoulder, bent to whisper in his ear, firmly admonishing, "You're too nice. You can't be nice like that, son. He'll run right over you to the goal and you'll be flat on your back. You don't have to hurt him or knock him over, but you've got to stop him. Next time, pull his shirt. Come up close. Next to him." As he talked he demonstrated by tugging on the hem at the back of the boy's shirt. He pulled again on his shirt, this time harder. The boy nodded slowly, not quite understanding.

PART ONE

A LIKELY STORY

1

———◆———

JUDITH THORNTON WAS doing her grocery shopping. There were a number of other things she could have been doing instead. She could have been reading the newspaper she hadn't been able to get to all day. She could have been doing the laundry or watching the news or reading the files she'd brought home from work. Those were the options, but options without choice. There was no milk in the refrigerator and there was no bread. Or butter.

Judith had been consciously trying to organize her spending, going to the store once a week instead of two or three times. She felt she needed to compensate somehow for the increase in her shameful adjustable mortgage and the rising costs of caring for a mother whose dementia had progressively rendered her mute and paraplegic. Her former husband Steven might be willing to increase his child support, but he was already paying far more than the court-ordered amount.

It wasn't as though she didn't have a fine job. As chief assistant in the San Diego District

Attorney's Office, she was making just over $100,000 a year. But with a four-thousand-dollar-a-month house payment, gardeners for the acre of grass surrounding the house, and house-related costs of over a thousand dollars a month, there wasn't much left for discretionary income. It bothered her at times that she paid as much to live in the house each month as some people got paid every two months. Yet she'd convinced herself the difficulty would pass.

Tonight Judith had taken the route along the darkened residential streets, avoiding the freeway. When she arrived at the store, the parking lot was nearly empty, the uniformed security guard leaning on the edge of a planter, smoking a cigarette.

Judith parked her car under one of the lights closest to the store entrance and stepped outside. A cool breeze blew her black velour sweatsuit against her thin body. She reached into her pants pocket for the grocery list she'd been compiling over the last few days. It wasn't there. She looked in her purse. It wasn't there either. Thinking it must have fallen from her pocket, Judith opened the driver's side door and looked under the seat. It wasn't to be found. She had to have dropped it somewhere between the house and the car. Had she put it in her pocket? She remembered having it in her hand. At the sink. It was folded in half, then folded a second time. How could she forget it?

Judith moved quickly through the store, trying to remember what was on the list, finally pushing the cart into the vegetable and fruit section.

The peaches looked ripe. The strawberries, they were a risky proposition. She never knew how ripe they were until she unpacked them at home. The lighting in the produce department must, she swore, be designed to make colors artificially brighter. So the orange strawberries looked ruby red and the white peaches looked ripe yellow. She picked up a basket of large strawberries and turned it over, inspecting the ones on the bottom. Across the bin, a woman in her seventies was watching her. Their eyes met for a moment and the woman shook her head. Judith nodded and put the strawberries back.

Judith moved quickly from stall to stall, the mound of food growing. When the ten-pound bag of potatoes lay heavy across the handle, she maneuvered the cart to the check stand and began unloading the groceries. She hated this part of grocery shopping, almost as much as having to carry the bags from the car to the kitchen, then unload everything.

"Paper or plastic, ma'am?" the bagger, a plump girl with frizzy red hair, asked as the pile of foods moved automatically across the black conveyor belt to the electronic counter that read the bar codes.

"Plastic's fine."

Somewhere in the middle of her response Judith remembered something. It was her driver's license. She wasn't sure she had it with her. She'd taken it out that afternoon and copied the number for the county driving form she needed to fill out every year in order to drive the county cars. She didn't need to take it out of the plastic folder it was in. Yet she had. And now she was certain it lay on her desk at work. She needed it to cash her check here. One glance into her wallet confirmed her fears.

Judith stared blankly at the checker and regretted she didn't recognize the woman. She knew several of the checkers well. This one was obviously new, and to her Judith was any other woman about to try to cash a check without proper identification.

Judith tried to sound spontaneous. "I forgot my driver's license."

When there appeared no look of sympathy on the checker's face, Judith offered, "I'm a deputy district attorney, you can find me if there's any problem . . . and there really won't be."

A twinge of guilt made her face flush red. She'd violated one of her own cardinal rules: she never used her position to curry favor anywhere. But it was almost 11:30 and she relished neither the humiliating thought of abandoning the order of food now almost totally checked and bagged nor the idea of having the store hold the groceries while she drove down to her office to retrieve the license. The last option wasn't possible anyway. The store closed at midnight and that was now only fifteen minutes away. She'd never make it back from the office in time.

As Judith struggled with her dwindling options, a man's voice broke the tension.

"Hey, Jude! Is that you?"

Only three people ever called her "Jude." And one of them, Aaron Mercer, was standing behind her, looking as if he'd just stepped off the golf course in his pale blue polo shirt and white cotton pants. Mercer's voice was deep, resonant. He was an aristocratic-looking man with silver-white hair and an austere, all-knowing demeanor. At six feet, even when she wore heels, he still towered above Judith. They must have made a stark contrast, she thought, she in her black velour pant suit and the tennis shoes she used for gardening, Mercer in his impeccable golfing attire.

"This lady is indeed a deputy district attorney. In fact, she's *the* chief assistant of the San Diego District Attorney's Office!" He didn't smile when he made the pronouncements. Undoubtedly he recognized the seriousness of her plight. Yet he was insensitive to maintaining her privacy, speaking so loudly the couple in the next checking aisle turned and stared at her, and her velour outfit.

Judith winced. Mercer and she were not friends, despite their five-year relationship together at the District Attorney's Office. She understood his feelings toward her. When Lawrence Farrell had become the district attorney, he'd moved Mercer from the Major Violator Unit to director of the Child Protection Division. It was Judith who was moved to the prestigious position of chief assistant. While Mercer hadn't expressed dissatisfaction, it was no secret he'd coveted the position Judith now held. And there were many who thought it was Mercer, not Judith, who should have been given the post.

Mercer was a trial attorney with razor-sharp ability. He was older than Judith by fifteen years. He also had ten years' more trial experience than she, and perhaps, most important, he was part of the office's old-boy network that had been quite cozy until Farrell's appointment and the unorthodox selection of a young woman to be his chief assistant. Shortly after her appointment, Mercer had begun addressing her as "Jude." He realized, of course, that no one ever called her "Jude." It was a purposeful breach of personal protocol designed solely to irritate her, and his references to her title now were no accident. He was going out of his way to embarrass her. He was smooth, even genteel, about it, but his style was unmistakable. Judith felt her face turn red as the punishment continued.

"And she's a struggling parent just trying to make ends meet. You can trust her," he bellowed at the clerk. "I will personally vouch for her integrity. In fact, if necessary, I'll cover the order. Tell me how much it is."

The store clerk eyeballed Judith's face as she stared back, expressionless and exhausted.

"Just a moment, I'll be right back." The clerk left the register and huddled with a short, black-haired man with a thin ferretlike face who Judith surmised was the store's night manager. As they waited, the people in line at the check stands next to them saw their food items rung up, bagged, and carried outside to waiting cars.

Mercer fidgeted and sighed audibly, grinding the humiliation in even further.

"Hope my Dreyers doesn't melt."

He shifted his half gallon of ice cream, the only item he was buying, from one hand to the other. Judith winced again and struggled to smile. He wasn't making her predicament any easier.

With the store manager and clerk still in deep conversation, Judith turned to Mercer.

"Aaron, if that one's melting, why don't you go exchange it for another and I'll hold your place?"

"Thanks, Jude!" As Mercer turned from the line and headed toward the freezer section at the back of the store, the clerk returned, holding out a pen to Judith.

"We'll accept your check if you put your work address and phone number on the front."

A wave of relief spread over Judith and with it a feeling of defeat. She complied as a woman with a cartful of groceries moved into line behind her, taking Mercer's place. Judith looked around. Hers was now the only check stand open. She could see Mercer at the back of the store, waving at her. He was on his way back, ready to check out. With all aisles except hers now down in preparation for the store closing, the line behind Judith had grown even longer as the people left in the store hurried to check out.

Judith pretended not to see Mercer's gesturing. She thanked the clerk and pushed her grocery cart toward the exit doors, leaving the now last-in-line Mercer holding his new carton of ice cream and looking for all the world as if it would melt before he got out of the store. She could feel his eyes follow her as she hurried out the doors to her car. It was an escape of sorts, Judith hoping she could load the groceries and drive away before he reached his car, the black Mercedes parked only two spaces from her blue Volvo.

The streets were nearly deserted as Judith drove back to her house. The small coffee shop at the corner of Adams Avenue was closing and the movie theater marquee was dark. She regretted what she'd done to Mercer. Although the humor wasn't lost on her, it was a mean act, and no matter how much he deserved it, no matter how much the moment of retaliation invigorated an otherwise disastrous encounter, what she'd done was beneath her. She resolved to offer some kind of explanation to Mercer if the opportunity presented itself the next day, although just what that might be was for the moment left somewhat vague.

Once home, Judith faced the chore of putting the groceries away. Before doing that she walked down the long hallway to Elizabeth's room. Her daughter was sleeping soundly. She backtracked down the hallway past the kitchen to the maid's quarters to her mother's room.

Her mother was still awake, staring up at the ceiling.

The noise Judith made moving through the house wakened Jeanne, her mother's aide. Until the previous month, Jeanne had been only a day worker, but suddenly there was a need for increased care. Fearing her mother would need her in the middle of the night and she would be at the other end of the house, too far away to assist, Judith had hired the health aide to sleep over four nights a week. When Judith worked late, she willingly doubled as a baby-sitter for Elizabeth.

The hiring of Jeanne on a twenty-four-hour basis hadn't been due to any perceived emergency. And it wasn't that her mother's physical condition had weakened. It was more subtle. There was a different look on her face. Her brow would knit as Judith helped turn her over to dress her. Something had changed, and Judith needed another presence in the house to help deal with it.

Judith's growing discomfort with her mother's condition also prompted her to call the San Diego Hospice telephone number she kept taped to her phone. The hospice nurses had come to the house a year earlier, when her mother's doctors had opined that she had less than a year to live. Under those circumstances the hospice health care was available—the requirement being the one-year survival estimate. After six months of hospice care, however, her mother was showing no signs of weakening. In fact, much to her doctor's surprise, she'd grown a bit stronger and was holding steady. In such a stabilized condition, the hospice nurses recommended her mother be eased out of the program to preserve the remaining year on the hospice coverage.

Now, however, there was an inexplicable

feeling of impending doom, and Judith, without being able to articulate a reason clearly, asked the hospice to return and reevaluate her mother. Judith had learned that in the world of medical care it was sometimes only intuition that formed the basis for treatment. The hospice staff responded to feelings, and Judith liked that. The supervising nurse had come out seven days earlier and promised to return in a week. That would make the next visit tomorrow.

"Are you okay, Mrs. Thornton?"

Judith nodded to Jeanne, who'd come out of her bedroom area. "I just needed to stop at the store for a few things."

"You want me to help put things away?"

"No, you go on back to sleep. I'll take care of this stuff."

Jeanne retreated to the bedroom once again and Judith began unpacking the groceries. By the time they were all put away, it was well after midnight. If her mother was still awake, she'd want a snack.

Judith looked in the cupboard, then the icebox, finally settling on a cup of strawberry yogurt, which she opened and carried into the bedroom.

The old woman's face was turned toward the door, and as Judith entered, she opened her eyes.

Judith knelt next to the bed, the yogurt cup in one hand, a teaspoon in the other. She held the yogurt at eye level. She couldn't be exactly sure how well her mother could see. Six months earlier the doctor had visited the house and after examining her, announced she'd lost most of the sight in her right eye. Until the doctor's visit, Judith hadn't suspected blindness. By now, perhaps her sight was totally gone. Judith tried to put the thought from her mind. As it was, she knew she'd been spending far too little time with her mother. The thought of her being locked away in a darkening world only added to the growing guilt that came with Judith's inability to control the uncontrollable.

"Hi, Mom," Judith whispered. "I thought you might be hungry, so I brought you some strawberry yogurt."

There were only two responses Judith was used to seeing if she offered food to her mother. She either ate it or she closed her eyes. Closing her eyes meant she didn't want to eat. It was a small physical sign, one that Judith had come to understand, one that in perhaps some small way verified there was still a consciousness in the woman, a consciousness the medical profession denied was there, denied because they could not deal with it, could not treat it. Judith suspected it made the doctors feel better by believing there was nothing left of her mother's thought processes. And in a perverse way, their reassurance of emptiness comforted her as well. It allowed her to bear all this, too, and allowed her to believe her mother was also free from the realization a slow death was upon her.

So her mother's reaction to the offer of food tonight startled her. She neither closed her eyes nor allowed Judith to feed her the small spoonfuls of yogurt. Instead, she uttered a low, guttural growl. Then she turned her head away from Judith.

Judith rose, put the yogurt on the nightstand and sat down on the bed, next to her mother.

A frightening thought welled up inside her as she saw a grimace spread across the woman's wrinkled face. It was a look of misery.

Judith caught her breath and searched for words.

The worst possibility was unfolding, shattering the safety of ignorance with which they'd all surrounded themselves.

"It's okay, Mom," Judith whispered. "It's all going to be okay."

The pinched expression on her mother's face faded as her muscles relaxed. Judith pulled the covers up to the woman's shoulders. She ran her hand through the woman's white hair and rested it on her shoulder; then she rose and walked to the foot of the bed, where she stood looking at her mother.

Why had she said those words, *Everything's fine?* Whatever could have possessed her to tell the woman such a thing?

Nothing was fine.

Nothing was the way anyone would want it.

Her declaration had been compelled by something, but it made no sense.

As she watched the woman breathing so shallowly, looking so sorrowful, so pitiful, the pain and anxiety stored in silence layer on layer for the last two years came crashing inward.

If there was a God, this wouldn't happen. If there was a God, you'd let her go; you wouldn't allow her to suffer like this. Who would let her stay on like this?

She paused as the surge of emotion shook loose another realization. She'd answered her own question. *Maybe it was her mother. Maybe her mother didn't want to die.* The thoughts came faster now. Why? The answer had been inside Judith all along. She'd said it out loud for her mother without knowing why she was saying it. But it was there, unrecognized. There, waiting to spill out. Her mother was waiting for her, for Judith, to tell her it was okay if she died. Waiting for someone to tell her everything was the way she wanted it to be and she could leave in peace. Waiting for someone to set her soul at rest.

God had nothing to do with it.

Judith could feel herself being pulled down, struggling against what she'd refused to see for many months.

This was the end. This was the moment Judith had to give permission. To her mother. To herself. She lingered at the bedside, watching her mother's face. Then she crossed to the windows and sat down on the bed, brushing back her mother's straw white hair as the old woman slept. She lowered her face and rested her cheek on her mother's.

"I love you, Mom. I love you. It's okay. It's all okay. It's up to you. When you want to leave us, whenever you want to leave us, it's okay. Elizabeth and I will be fine."

She began to cry, the tears dripping from her cheeks to the pillow before she could compose herself.

Within minutes her mother's shallow breathing assured her the woman was asleep. There was nothing more she could do. She rose and turned off the lights.

Judith covered the uneaten cup of yogurt with plastic wrap and placed it in the refrigerator. She was exhausted and wanted to fall into bed. The files she'd brought home to review could wait until morning. But there were only two of them and if she waited until morning they'd be competing with her time for Elizabeth. She glanced at her wristwatch. It was 12:35. An hour and a cup of hot tea. They were all she needed.

The light in the wood-paneled office library was still on. The two files lay in the center of the desk. Both were child molest cases, and Farrell wanted her advice on whether there was sufficient evidence to charge the suspects with crimes. More important, both were cases Aaron Mercer, as head of the Child Protection Division, felt should be prosecuted. After what she'd done to him tonight, she felt she owed him a timely and complete review. If she was going to disagree with him, she needed to have solid reasons.

Normally, Judith would not have been placed in a position to second-guess Mercer, but Farrell was locked in a close reelection campaign. A centerpiece of his opponent's platform was his criticism of Farrell for not adequately prosecuting child molesters. Although Farrell was usually not bothered by public criticism, he took his opponent's comments seriously. He'd been stung by a repeat offender's mutilation murder of a second victim. Seven years earlier, the man, Brady Hawthorne, had sexually assaulted a young girl. Farrell, then chief deputy district attorney, had negotiated a plea bargain which had allowed the man to serve only half his sentence in prison. A month ago, just three weeks after his release from prison, Hawthorne was arrested for the murder of a second girl, this time an eight-year-old. It was not being taken lightly by the press, and Farrell was second-guessing himself on every close case. The two cases he'd sent over to Judith were cases he had doubts about, but in both Aaron Mercer thought there should be prosecution.

In the first case, the evidence was weak, but there was an eyewitness who'd made a tentative identification of the defendant. The identification was full of holes and the witness hadn't been able to identify the suspect at a jailhouse lineup. Still, it was the kind of case you let the jury decide. Judith typed a short note and stapled it to the outside of the file. Bottom line: she agreed with Mercer.

The second case was far more difficult. Thomas Russell, a forty-five-year-old auto mechanic, was charged with sexually abusing his own child. That alone made Judith stop and think before reading on. She was used to seeing sexual abuse cases, many within the victim's immediate family. But the usual scenario was abuse by an ex-boyfriend of the mom's. Or a current live-in boyfriend. Not many involving the natural father.

Then there was the girl herself. She was consistently denying that her father abused her. Yet her story was a strange, even bizarre one. According to her, she said she'd been sleeping when a man had come through her bedroom window, woken her up, and carried her outside. He'd supposedly driven her to get an ice cream before assaulting her. The summary of reports in the file made it clear the medical professionals and social workers who'd interviewed her didn't believe her story. Neither did Aaron Mercer. Yet stranger factual scenarios had, upon investigation, turned out to be true.

It was 1 A.M. Where there'd been exhaustion thirty minutes earlier, there was now curiosity of an urgent nature. It occurred to Judith that the girl might be telling the truth.

Judith pulled the social agency file. The girl was in a foster home. The father was in jail. If the man hadn't molested the girl, if she'd been telling the truth, and the entire family had been pulled apart. . . .

Judith started with the handwritten report from the doctor who was the first to examine Caryn. She'd told him the same story that appeared throughout the file, adding that the man who came through the window was a little taller than her mother and was wearing a black uniform and had spots all over his face. He'd told her he'd return and kill her family if she told anyone he'd been there.

The next report was the one from the first police detective to interview Caryn. It was the only report to describe the kidnapper's vehicle, which Caryn said was big and black, with a license plate that had mountains on it.

Judith was most interested in the final report from the social worker, who'd recommended that Caryn be placed in a foster home. The social worker, Delma Travers, had urged the placement to assure the child adequate protection. She wrote: "It is far better to err on the side of the child's safety than risk possible future injury to the child." No doubt, Delma Travers's recommendation that the case be handled as a child abuse matter had played a major role in Caryn's being removed from the Russell home.

Next, Judith read through the reports to see whether Tom Russell had been cooperative with the investigators. He'd agreed to supply blood and skin scrapings, demanded a lie detector test, and insisted on seeing his daughter. The request for visitation had been denied on the grounds that it would upset the girl too much. From that point on, his level of cooperation had deteriorated.

After an hour of reading through the Russell file, Judith was even more unwilling to dismiss Caryn's version of events. It was not altogether impossible. Her explanation of what had happened and the sequence of events was the same every time she'd been asked to restate them. Even when asked directly, the girl was adamant that the assailant was not her father.

There was another report Judith wanted to scan. Forensics. The subsequent search of the Russell house revealed no evidence of guilt. The evidence collected in and around Caryn's bedroom, including her bed sheets and her nightgown, were being tested. In addition, the report pointed out that Tom Russell showed the police scrape marks around the girl's bedroom windowsill. The report referred to these marks as "inconclusive."

Tests. Where were the medical lab tests on Tom Russell? Judith paged through the file and found the police lab sheets. Tom Russell had indeed voluntarily given blood and urine samples in order to exclude him from the group of individuals who could have assaulted Caryn. The medical tests were negative on drugs and alcohol at the time of the test. That meant nothing when it came to whether he'd been under the influence fourteen hours earlier.

The current status report on the parties was at the end of the child welfare agency paperwork. Caryn was being detained in a foster home. Russell had been charged with molesting his daughter and was still in jail on $200,000 bail. Things couldn't be much worse for them—except for the fact that it was Aaron Mercer who'd initiated the charges. The Russells were hardly likely to find any sympathy in him.

Judith closed the file and placed it at the corner of her desk. If it were her call, she'd have waited to arrest Tom Russell. There was scant evidence against him. And what evidence there was didn't impress her.

She took a notepad of white lined paper from the desk drawer and composed a short handwritten memo to Mercer and Farrell expressing her view that Thomas Russell just might be innocent.

It was Elizabeth, dressed and ready for school, who awakened Judith the following morning. She'd forgotten to set the alarm, and at the sight of Elizabeth, Judith had leaped from bed.

Her head was throbbing as she stuffed the Russell file into her briefcase, reminded now that she was about to take on Mercer's evaluation of the case. She wanted the memo to reach Mercer and Farrell's desks before the trial calendar began at 8:30. After that it would be hard to find Mercer in his office until the courts broke for lunch at noon. By then she was hoping they would have a chance to discuss the case.

As Elizabeth picked up her school backpack and walked through the laundry room to the garage, Judith walked to her mother's bedroom door. Jeanne was already awake and setting her clothes out for the day.

Judith looked toward her mother's bed. The woman was propped up with four pillows, slumped awkwardly to the right, her jaw slack, her mouth slightly open. Judith didn't enter the room but instead yelled from the doorway.

"'Bye, Mom. I'm late. I'll be back at one-thirty."

The old woman's eyes shifted to her daughter. Judith turned and hurried into the garage, recognizing in herself only the slightest feeling of discomfort. This morning there was something different in her mother's eyes. Were they discolored? She'd been too far away. But they were different. It was the color. They weren't as white.

As she rounded the corner to Fairmount Avenue and drove toward the freeway, Judith had an inexplicable, gnawing regret. *I should have hugged her good-bye. Why didn't I just take the thirty seconds to hug her good-bye?*

Judith's first task at the office was to drop her memo off with both Mercer's and Farrell's secretaries. She was glad neither man was at his desk. She wouldn't have to spar verbally with Mercer, and she preferred Farrell see her arguments in writing before discussing them with him.

She worked until 10 o'clock and broke for coffee, returning at 10:30. As soon as she walked through the office door, she knew something was wrong. She'd been a deputy in the office for over ten years. When a person worked in a place that long, they could walk into it and know when there was something wrong. It was an air, vibrations, the way people acknowledged or didn't acknowledge your presence. Call it what one wished, it was on the faces of the secretaries this morning.

Judith passed Susan Middleton's desk. The secretary fumbled with the long blond curls hanging over the front of her shoulders. As Judith passed by, Susan averted her eyes, suddenly immersed in her work. At the pencil sharpener, she stopped. Andrea Bracken, Aaron Mercer's secretary, was standing there, a pile of sharpened pencils on the table next to her, a box of unsharpened pencils in her hand.

"What in heaven's name are you doing, Andrea?" Judith asked. "You've got to have at least twenty-five pencils sharpened there."

"Mr. Mercer wants them sharpened," she replied meekly, looking down at the growing pile of orange wood.

A note of sarcasm accompanied Judith's inquiry. "All of them?"

"Yeah, all of them. He's going to trial, and, well, he likes the way I sharpen his pencils."

Judith stepped closer to the secretary.

"What else is going on, Andrea? The place has a pretty cool quality this morning."

The secretary's eyes shifted right and left, gauging where the rest of the office workers were and how close. Perceiving herself safe from other ears, she leaned toward Judith. "It's Mr. Mercer. He's got a couple of us reading a manuscript for him."

"What do you mean, he's got a couple of you reading a manuscript for him?" Judith whispered back.

The secretary again scanned the area around her. "It's this trial he's working on. There's a case like it on appeal from our office, and he has a transcript of that trial. He's called at least three of us in to read parts of it, and at least with me, he's asked what I thought of what I'd read."

"And? What did you think?"

"Actually, Mrs. Thornton, the stuff was pretty raunchy."

"Raunchy how?"

"Ah . . . well . . . I'd rather not talk about it. That's why people are so quiet here this morning. No one knows who's going to be called in to read next."

Her curiosity piqued, Judith asked, "If I got a hold of the transcript, would you show me what you were asked to read?"

"I'd rather do that than try to remember what I read in there."

Their conversation was interrupted by the opening of Mercer's office door. Karen Belski, the office's newest secretary, quickly exited, her face red.

Andrea looked at the fleeing woman, then cast a knowing glance toward Judith.

"I'd like to see that transcript. Can you see I get it, with the places marked that you've been reading back?" Judith asked.

Andrea was about to answer when Mercer came through his office door and yelled.

"Judith! Just the person I wanted to see." He waved her toward him. "Can you come in for a moment?"

"Be right there," Judith called back. Then turning to Andrea, she added, "Bet he doesn't ask me to read."

"Don't count it out," the secretary whispered back to her.

Judith crossed the office to Mercer's doorway.

"Come on in, Judith, and have a seat."

Mercer stood behind his desk, his arms folded across his chest. The greeting sounded sincere enough, but she knew he was dealing not only with the memo she'd left expressing her sharp disagreement on the Russell case, but also with the embarrassment of their encounter in the grocery store the previous night. Best to get this over quickly, she thought.

"No, thanks. I'll stand. Look, Aaron, about last night . . . at the grocery store. . . ."

She sounded awkward, too apologetic, and she caught herself, allowing him to continue.

"No problem, Judith. Really. All's fair in the lines, so to speak."

She would pursue the matter no further than a brief apology. "No, really, Aaron, I'm sorry I. . . ."

"We don't have to discuss it, Judith. Actually, I'm far more interested in *this.*"

As he spoke he reached toward the corner of his desk, picking up a memo she recognized at once as the one she'd written on the Russell case, the one she'd dropped off earlier that morning.

"Can we talk about this, Judith?" he asked, setting the memo on the desk again, letting it go slightly above the wood so it floated downward, toward her. His inflection and the manner in which he redeposited it were intended as a clear signal he'd rejected its conclusion.

"You disagree." Judith's response was a flat understatement.

"Of course I do. I was the one who put the man in jail."

"There's not enough evidence to put this man in jail, Aaron."

"Perhaps you'd like to read over the police reports?"

"I have, Aaron. And they haven't changed my mind a bit. There's no evidence Tom Russell assaulted his own daughter. Not a shred of evidence. I'd be happy to consider any, if you could point it out to me. All I see is that he had an opportunity to do it because he was there. In my book, that's not enough. The bedroom window, after all, *was unlocked.*"

"But the girl's story doesn't make sense."

Judith smiled. "You don't have children, do you, Aaron?"

He drew his shoulders back slightly.

"Kids tell the truth sometimes, they really do," she said. "What's so unusual about an assault by someone coming through a window? We've had plenty of entries through unlocked windows. Burglaries, rapes. Murder."

"It's not the crime, Judith, it's the rest of her story. He carried her outside? Took her out for ice cream? Really!"

It was a subtle put-down. It was the tone of his voice that added, *How could you be so naive?*"

"Look, Aaron, if we're wrong . . . if we've arrested a man for a crime he didn't commit . . . and we've ripped that family apart in the process. . . . Where's the girl now?"

"She's in a foster home."

Judith shook her head. "My God, Aaron."

"I can't persuade you on this?"

"No, you can't. Not on this one."

"I guess Larry makes the call, then."

"He's going to have to."

Then Mercer's tone—and tactics—changed. The voice was lower, mellow, and the innuendo clear. "You *know*, Larry's got a tough election ahead."

It was true. Farrell was running hard for reelection on a "get tough on sexual predators and child molesters" platform. His opponent, a former deputy district attorney, found a case to use against him, one that as a young deputy, Farrell had plea-bargained down from rape to sexual battery on a minor. The guy had been released early and killed another child, a nine-year-old. When it had happened, the newspapers hadn't been kind to Farrell or the district attorney's office. Now, in the heat of a political fight, his opponent was being even less kind, finding every opportunity to demagogue the case. He'd even brought an enlarged photo of the dead girl to the press conference at which he'd announced his candidacy.

Farrell was trying his best to respond to the criticism, trying to explain that the evidence in the case had been weak and they'd have been lucky to bring in a verdict of any kind, trying to tell the public the plea bargain had at least kept him off the street for a while. But such intricate matters of trial tactics and policy weren't easily explained to the public. All the public could digest was that a man had assaulted a little girl, had got out too early, and had done it again, this time killing another little girl.

"What's the election got to do with whether there's enough evidence to charge Tom Russell with sexually assaulting his own child?"

"Everything, Judith. It's an issue."

Judith's voice rose slightly. "No, it's not, Aaron. It's got nothing to do with it." There was silence before she spoke again. "I'm going to the mat on this one, Aaron."

Mercer stepped out from behind his desk and moved to within a foot or two of her, his eyes tracing her body, feet to face. "I'd enjoy that."

Judith caught her breath and held it. Her knees weakened. She struggled to put a label on the surge of surprise and anger. She said nothing. If his comment, his physical intrusion, were calculated to disarm her, he'd been successful. She instinctively took a step away.

"Why not see Larry?" Mercer cooed. "He's in, I know. I was talking to him before you came in."

Judith was able to manage only a cryptic, "I guess we should. I have a staff meeting at noon."

Farrell didn't look up as Mercer, followed at a distance by Judith, walked into his office.

Farrell hadn't waited for them to explain their positions. "Well, have the two of you reached any agreement on the Russell case?" His greeting was perfunctory, which meant he was unhappy. Judith could see her memo lying on his desk, slightly to the right of the one he was reading.

"You know I prefer my assistants work out these charging issues themselves."

Mercer responded first, leaving Judith, for the moment, unable to defend her position.

"I've set out my own concerns for Judith, but I don't think I've persuaded her."

"That right, Judith?"

"That's about it, Larry. It's all there in my memo to you. There's not one solid piece of evidence to charge Russell with an assault on his daughter, not one piece of evidence."

"There's plenty there," Mercer protested. "The girl's made up an incredible story to protect her father. Her father and mother were the only adults in the house with her."

Farrell picked Judith's memo from the desk. "I've read Judith's memo, and I've chatted with you, Aaron. Frankly, I think Judith has the better argument. We don't have the tests yet. The DNA results are going to take six to eight weeks. He's not going to go anywhere if we wait on the charges."

"I'm talking about more than the tests, Larry. What if we make a mistake on this one? What if we let this guy go and he hurts this girl, or some other girl? The press would be. . . ."

Judith interrupted. "What the press does isn't relevant. This is a prosecutorial decision. It ought to be based on the facts of the case. Only the facts of the case." She looked at Farrell. "The political fallout from some other case isn't relevant, Larry. You know it's not."

"What if Aaron's right and we make a wrong call on this one? If we let this guy out and he does it again? Do we run that risk here?"

"We always run that risk. Why don't we ask that little girl whose father's in jail? Why not ask her if we should arrest her father? That is, if someone will tell us what foster home they've stuck her in."

Mercer ignored the sarcasm. "I say we charge him and we go forward with the case."

"I can't tell you how strongly I feel about this, Larry. Charging an innocent man? It's the most unethical thing I can think of." Something inside her snapped. Perhaps it was a reaction to Mercer. The worst possible standoff. Putting herself on the line. But she couldn't stop herself. "I can't imagine working in an office that would do such a thing."

Silence followed as Judith turned and walked out, leaving the two men to absorb the import of her comment.

Her heart was pounding as she walked down the hallway to her office and sat at her desk. For a moment Judith stared blankly at the copy of her memo, now partially buried under the case files that had arrived while she was in Farrell's office. She'd backed herself into a corner and issued an ultimatum without exactly being sure why. It was, she realized at once, a case of overkill.

She opened the center drawer and removed all the pens and pencils. Now what? Had she really threatened to quit if the charges against

Russell weren't dropped? Before she could answer the question, she heard Farrell's voice.

"You're not leaving, Judith?"

She looked up and saw him standing in the doorway.

"Who says I'm not?"

He walked toward her. "I say you're not. I told Aaron you're handling the case. The person who handles this one calls the shots. The guy's in custody. You can let him post bail. But can you at least wait until the tests are in before you dismiss all charges? It's not what you might want to do right now, but it's a compromise. And if it's dismissed, I'd sure like to be able to give the press a good reason or two."

"Thanks, Larry. I don't know what I'd have done if you hadn't come down here."

He sighed and stepped away from the door. "I'm afraid you'd have done what you said you were going to do. Put those pencils away, will you? You're making me nervous."

"What did Aaron say?"

As Farrell strode away, he looked over his shoulder at Judith, "Nothing you want to hear."

Judith stared down at her plate. The gold rim around the cream-colored china blurred and she felt her body falling forward toward the restaurant table. She'd momentarily lost her balance.

"Are you okay?"

Andrew Weiss was one of the newest associates in the office. This was his first staff lunch with the more experienced attorneys who met weekly to compare notes and share information on the cases they were assigned.

Judith straightened herself and looked up at the clock on the restaurant wall. It was 1:40. She'd promised her mother she'd be home at 1:30 to check on her, and she still needed to drop off Elizabeth's flute at school for her lesson after classes. She had no cases of her own set for the afternoon calendar, and if she left now, she could be back in the office by 2:45.

As Judith picked up her purse from the floor under her chair and stood, Andrew frowned.

"Are you really sure you're okay, Judith?"

"Of course I am. Don't I look okay?"

"No, not really," he insisted. "Are you dizzy?"

"Always," she smiled back, removing a ten-dollar bill from her wallet and handing it to him. "I think this'll cover my lunch."

As she left the restaurant, Judith glanced at the wall clock again. It was 1:45. There was a feeling driving her to move quickly, an intuition something was wrong somewhere. She needed to be home.

No sooner had the garage door automatically closed behind Judith's car, than Jeanne stepped through the door connecting the garage to the house. Wringing her hands and shaking her head, she walked quickly toward Judith.

"She's gone, Mrs. Thornton. They took her."

Jeanne's response made no sense. "Gone where?" Judith demanded.

"She's gone."

Her mother had had a seizure, perhaps. Was in the hospital. Judith quickened her pace, passing Jeanne and heading toward her mother's room. But as she stepped into the laundry room she was confronted by a woman she immediately recognized, the hospice nurse who'd promised to return today. Judith stopped abruptly.

"Where's my mother?" Judith whispered.

The nurse was gentle but direct. "Your mother died about forty-five minutes ago, Mrs. Thornton." She looked toward the bedroom, indicating she was still in the house.

Judith hurried to the bedroom door and stopped. The nurse walked past her now and stood at the foot of the bed looking at her mother, noticing for the first time that the nurse was holding a small towel, briskly wiping her hands, and looking at her mother the way an artist looks at a canvas he's just completed. Her mother lay in a pink bed robe, her hair combed and her hands placed across her chest.

Judith held her breath. Every line of pain etched into the old woman's face was gone, as were the stiff body and the ever-present washcloths clenched in her hands. Every muscle tensed to grotesque rigidity had relaxed. She had the appearance of a woman asleep. Whatever had come in the hours before, there was in the aftermath, at this moment, no delineation between life and death.

Judith turned to the nurse.

"She looks . . ." Judith wanted to say she looked beautiful, but it was so out of place, so wrong to say it. Yet it was true. Death had lifted a veil of physical torture and left in its place a peacefulness Judith had not seen for years.

"Can I be alone with her?"

"Of course." The nurse reached out and touched Judith's elbow. "Can I get you something?"

"No. No, thank you," Judith whispered. Then she said something she'd remember forever. After she said it, she realized it must have sounded so very strange to the nurse. Yet she could offer no explanation for it then and never would.

"I just need some time with her. I've been waiting for this for so long. . . ."

The nurse didn't react to her statement but closed the bedroom door and went to the kitchen.

Alone with her mother, Judith knelt at the side of the bed and placed her cheek against her mother's still warm skin. Only the tip of her nose was cold.

She was able to remain at the bedside for only a few minutes. Then Judith needed to move, to get up and walk. Her mind was spinning. She missed being home to see her mother when she said she would. She hadn't said good-bye, hadn't kept her promise. Yet what had been traded for the promise? Her first view of her mother's body, of death, was in repose, in peace. There was a gentle con-

frontation. This was certainly what her mother
would have wanted. It could not have been
planned more smoothly. Still . . . still. . . .

Judith found the nurse in the kitchen, hanging up the phone.

"I hope you don't mind, I took the liberty
of calling the funeral home you designated
when you filled out the hospice papers a year
ago. I don't think we need to call the coroner.
Your family doctor can certify your mother's
death as congestive heart failure. But we do
need to make the arrangements to remove her
body."

Judith sat at the breakfast table, then stood,
walked to the sink, and walked back to the
table again. She couldn't bring her body to rest
in any one place. She wanted to stop, wanted
her body to shut down and adjust, but everything else kept moving, going at its normal
pace. The result was a feeling she was moving
in slow motion.

"Thanks. . . . I appreciate your getting Mom
ready. . . ."

"No need to say anything. I'm glad I was
here at the right time." She smiled gently. "I
think your mom was waiting for me."

The last comment was lost on Judith as she
suddenly remembered Elizabeth was due
home in her carpool in an hour. "Can I keep
Mom here until Elizabeth comes home from
school? I think. . . ."

The nurse finished the thought. "Elizabeth
will need some closure here in the house. But
the funeral home's coming at five o'clock. You

really don't want your mother here much longer than that."

The nurse's beeper sounded and she walked to the phone and dialed. Several minutes later she returned to Judith.

"I have another call. I have to leave. Are you going to be all right?"

"I'll be fine, thank you. Jeanne's still here and I'll have her stay until Elizabeth says good-bye to her grandmother and the funeral home leaves."

"Can I call you later tonight and check on you?"

"Thanks. I'll be all right."

When she left, Judith sat at the kitchen table, dealing with the strange awareness that her mother lay dead in the next room.

Elizabeth hadn't taken her grandmother's death well. She'd demanded to see her, and Judith had obliged, walking with the girl into the bedroom, but then, not knowing quite what to say, she'd allowed Elizabeth to lead the conversation and stay in the room as long as she'd wanted. There was nothing she could say to make the situation any better for her or cushion the blow of her daughter seeing a dead person for the first time. Had she not allowed the girl to see her, there would not have been the closure the girl demanded and needed. The girl was too old to shield from death and too young to have to deal with it.

It was Elizabeth who raised the issue of where Judith's mother would be buried. Off and on over the last year, Judith had given the matter some thought but hadn't reached any decision. If the funeral was going to be held back in Ohio, with her family, in the church plots there, it would mean deciding if Elizabeth would go with her. She'd have some time to think about it overnight.

When the doorbell chimed, Judith gave Elizabeth a hug and sent her down to her room. But the girl hesitated. Looking up at Judith, she put her hand into her pants pocket and retrieved something she held out to her mother.

"What is it, Elizabeth?"

"It's for Grandma to take with her."

Judith's arm extended outward, her hand opened. Into it Elizabeth dropped a penny.

"It's for Grandma to take with her. Can you tell the people where she's going to put it under her pillow?"

As the doorbell chimed a second time, Judith knelt down and looked into Elizabeth's face, at the tears welled in her eyes and running onto her cheeks. For the first time Judith couldn't contain her own grief. Her arms reached around the now sobbing girl, and choking back her own sobs, she hugged her.

"Sure, baby, I'll give it to Grandma to take with her. It'll be her good luck penny."

She held Elizabeth a moment longer, until the doorbell chimed yet again and Elizabeth pulled away and walked down the hallway toward the bedroom.

Judith hurried to the front door and opened it. Two young men dressed in white coats and speaking in low, reverent tones introduced themselves as the representatives from the mortuary.

"What can I do to help?" Judith asked.

The shorter of the two men tried to reassure her. "Nothing, really, just relax while we get your mother safely into the van."

Judith held out her hand to him. "Can you put this under my mother's head? It's from my daughter. She says it's her grandmother's. . . ." Here she caught her breath. ". . . Her lucky penny."

From that point onward, Judith became a silent observer. She walked into the kitchen and poured a cup of coffee. As she stirred the sugar into the coffee, she could hear the men moving bed covers and lifting her mother onto the gurney. What was the right thing to do? There must be something else she should be doing besides drinking a cup of coffee. But she couldn't think of anything. Once, then twice and three times, there was the sound of metal hitting the wall. She knew it was the gurney. She'd heard the same sound hundreds of times as her mother's wheelchair struck the plaster and the wood door frames.

One of the men, again the shorter of the two, came into the kitchen.

"Mrs. Thornton?"

"Yes?"

"I'm sorry, we can't get the gurney out the side door."

Judith stood, facing the man, not knowing quite what to say.

When she didn't speak, he apologized. "I'm

sorry, we don't usually have these kinds of problems."

"Well, what do you think we ought to do? Mom doesn't seem to want to leave."

"I was thinking maybe the front door? Can we take her out the front way?"

"She'd probably prefer that."

The taller of the men went outside to drive the van to the front door, and this time Judith watched as the gurney with her mother on it was rolled down the hallway. For the first time she realized her mother was in a body bag. A white body bag. It was plastic. With a silver zipper on the side. Judith did not follow the gurney to the front door. Something stopped her, prevented her from watching any further.

Several minutes later the two men came back into the house and the shorter and more vocal of the two handed Judith the mortuary's card.

"Be sure to call first thing in the morning, Mrs. Thornton, and don't worry. Your mother'll be okay. We'll take good care of her. Just try to get some rest."

When they left the house, Judith walked to the dining room window overlooking the driveway and watched the van drive slowly down Tierra Verde. She walked down the hallway to Elizabeth's room and found the girl asleep in bed, her school clothes still on. Judith covered her and retraced her steps to the kitchen, then into her mother's room. Slowly at first, then more quickly, she stripped the bed of all the covers and sheets. She placed them with the pillows and carried the entire pile of linen outside, stuffed it in a large white plastic garbage bag, and stuffed the bag in the trash.

Judith slept shallowly, periodically awakening under the heavy bed covers, remembering it wasn't a bad dream, her mother was dead, lying in a small brown stucco building several miles away. In the moments she awakened, a mixture of strange, morbid thoughts plagued her. What was her mother's body lying on? Was she covered? What was she covered with? Did they put the pink flannel robe on her? What did her face, her eyes, her arms look like now? Were her eyes open, just a little? Was her hair a wild white, the way it was when she was asleep at home? Judith felt lost, suspended in a vacuum. There was no reserve of personal experience to fall back on, to remember. Nothing like this had ever happened to her before. There was a noise outside Judith's bedroom. Footsteps. Then a small body crawling into bed, under the covers, next to her. Neither Judith nor Elizabeth spoke. Judith pulled her close and fell into a deep, dreamless sleep.

At 7:30 the next morning Judith made the sad obligatory calls to her mother's family in Ohio. Her aunt cried, but all in all, the family seemed to take the news better than Judith had thought they would. Yes, they could arrange for the burial there. All Judith needed to do was make the transportation arrangements and they would take care of everything else. The mortuary that had buried two earlier generations of the family stood ready to accept her mother and prepare a fitting funeral. Would she be bringing Elizabeth? they wanted to know. They wanted to see her. They hadn't seen her since she was an infant. But Judith had already decided Elizabeth should stay in San Diego. She had school. She'd never been to a funeral before, and she didn't need the stress. Steven had already agreed she should stay with him.

At 8:30 the phone rang.

"Judith? It's Larry. I'm so sorry about your mother."

"Thanks, Larry. I'm going to need to take some time off to go back home to Ohio for the funeral."

"Take as much time as you need. Plan on two weeks and call me if you need more time. Aaron Mercer's already come in and volunteered to cover for you."

"Thank him for me, Larry. I appreciate the help." Then she remembered. "The only pressing case is the Russell case. Aaron's just going to have to use his best judgment when the tests come in. I wouldn't ever try to second-guess him, Larry, but I'd appreciate it if you could just be sure Russell doesn't slip through the cracks."

"Don't worry, Judith, he won't. Just don't worry about anything, okay?" He laughed gently. "I hate to tell you this, but you're expendable. You can take a break. The office is going to miss you, but we're not going to fall apart, honest. Visit your family and give me a call when you're ready to come back to work."

When she hung up, Judith telephoned the funeral home. Her mother's body was already scheduled to fly out of San Diego that night.

Judith called Steven to set the final plans for him to pick up Elizabeth and then began packing for the trip to Ohio.

2

JUDITH HAD DRIVEN El Cajon Boulevard thousands of times, never noticing the small mortuary seven minutes from her home. This morning she went prepared for the worst, even though she couldn't articulate just what the worst might be. She'd been to funerals but had never arranged one. From the moment she walked through the front entrance, every casket, every box, every room with an open door to look through was a breath-catching voice into which a momentary gaze might shake her soul or break her heart.

"Mrs. Thornton?"

A man in a dark gray suit emerged from a small office and approached, extending his hand to her.

"Samuel Barker. I'm the director of the funeral home. Won't you come in and have a seat?"

He ushered her into a small office and gestured to one of four lavender cloth-covered chairs.

"Can I get you something to drink?"

"Some water, I'd appreciate just some water."

He left and a moment later returned with a glass of water, which he set lightly before her, and then retreated to his own brown leather chair on the other side of the desk.

"I'd like to reassure you first that your wishes will be carried out exactly as you want them. When we spoke last, you indicated your mother will be buried in Canton, Ohio, and we've contacted the funeral home whose name you gave us. You need to provide them with whatever dress or outfit in which your mother will be buried. I'd suggest you take it back with you rather than try to send it, then you can take it directly to them. Your mother's already booked on a flight. . . ."

"I'm sorry," Judith interrupted, "how do you book her on a flight?"

"Well, it's a little awkward to explain, but . . . she'll be traveling in the cargo hold, it's . . . it's really the only way. . . ."

"Oh, that's okay," Judith reassured him, "I just . . . hadn't thought about the actual physical arrangements. Will she be in. . . ."

"Oh, of course, of course. We'll have you select a casket. . . ."

"I already have. The pink one I saw when I came in."

"Yes, it's a beautiful choice."

"What time will she be leaving for Ohio?"

"Tonight at ten P.M."

"The red eye."

"He smiled. "The red eye, yes."

"In the cargo hold?"

"In the cargo hold."

There was a moment of silence and he continued. "If you give me a moment to go through my file here, I need to run down the various costs and choices you have."

One by one he methodically read the items necessary for a proper transporting of the body and burial. At the end, he handed the list to Judith. She was a lawyer, and lawyers were supposed to read contracts carefully, but she scanned it quickly and signed at the bottom.

"I'm sure it's okay, Mr. Barker. It's all reasonable. Do you need a check now? I can. . . ."

"If you prefer, we can send it along to you."

"I'd appreciate that. That's all I have to do?"

He handed a copy of the invoice to her. "That's all. Just trust we'll take care of your mother."

As she rose to leave, Judith remembered. *The penny.* It was a small thing suddenly of immense importance.

"Oh, Mr. Barker, one more thing. My. . . ." Until that moment she'd been in control of her emotions, but inexplicably, her voice broke. ". . . My daughter sent along a. . . ." She couldn't go on. Choking back tears, her hand covered her mouth. She couldn't say it.

"She sent along a penny."

Judith nodded, daring not to utter a word lest the torrent of emotion so far held in check burst.

"It's with your mother now. We've placed it in an envelope, and I'll personally see it goes back with her."

Judith took a deep breath, extended her hand again, and while she wanted to say much more, wanted to express her gratitude for his attention to this small detail—the item of sudden consuming importance to her— managed only a weak, "Thank you."

By mid-afternoon Judith's suitcases were packed and she was at the Fashion Valley Mall, walking between rows of dresses. She'd decided to buy the funeral dress in California and not risk being unable to find what she wanted in some store she was unfamiliar with in Ohio.

There were summer florals hanging on the rack to her right, the kind that would have caught her mother's eye. She reached for a pink and blue one, pulling it out from the other dresses, spreading its hem to get a full look at the style and pattern.

"That's a beautiful dress!" The woman standing behind her glanced approvingly over Judith's shoulder. "The color'll look *wonderful* on you."

Judith answered without turning to look at the woman.

"It's not for me. It's for my mother."

"She'll love it, I'm sure!"

Judith let the hem of the dress fall against the rack and turned.

"I think she will," Judith said softly.

The woman nodded approvingly and walked away as Judith checked the dress label for the size. She supposed it wasn't critical, but it wasn't exactly irrelevant, either. It was a 14. Probably about right. She removed the dress on its hanger from the rack and carried it to the sales counter.

The sales clerk gushed approval of her choice as she took Judith's credit card.

"Can I get you a scarf, or perhaps a necklace to match?" the clerk asked.

"No, I don't think so," Judith replied.

"Earrings?"

"Not today, no."

"We're having a wonderful shoe sale. I'll bet you could find a pair to match this pink."

This would be the time, Judith thought, to tell her it was for a dead woman who was going to be buried in it, but she refrained. The clerk was trying to be helpful; it wasn't her fault. Most people come in looking for a dress for the living, to match their hair or eyes or personality. People didn't wander in shopping for a dead person. Oddly, though, it was no different than shopping for someone who was alive. She would be going through the same motions, the same conversation, if her mother was home watching television or sitting in the garden.

"No thanks, it's for my mom, and we're having her wear slippers with it."

It was true. Judith had decided her mother wasn't being buried with shoes on. Her feet wouldn't be showing in the casket, and besides, her mother hadn't worn shoes in several years.

The woman paused a moment. "Oh, but this dress just begs for a pair of sandals." The thought of someone wearing slippers with this fine dress had just been explained, but it would take a moment for the explanation to surface.

"I know, but . . . she . . . she hasn't worn shoes in . . . oh . . . two years," Judith added.

Catching the increasingly halting tone of Judith's voice, the urgency of the dress itself, the clerk offered more hesitantly, "Well . . . we do have lovely. . . ." But the look of increasing frustration on Judith's face, the way she pursed her lips and averted her eyes, stopped the clerk in mid-sentence as she realized the sale was over. There was silence before she added, "What if I just leave this on the hanger . . . so it won't get wrinkled?" Then, testing her own sudden feeling of frustration, she added, "Does it matter if it's wrinkled?"

Judith softened and in a hushed whisper of a voice offered, "That would be helpful . . . and it doesn't matter if you fold it."

The clerk chose not to remove the dress from the hanger. She covered it with a white plastic bag and came out from behind the counter to hand it to Judith, deliberately stepping in front of Judith to examine her face.

"Is there anything else I can do to help?"

Judith pursed her lips again and took the dress from the woman. She walked toward the exit, with a barely audible, "No, not a thing."

When she reached home, Judith carefully folded the dress and laid it on top of her own clothes in the largest of the two suitcases she was taking with her. Steven had picked up Elizabeth, and there was nothing more to do other than be sure Elizabeth got to her scheduled soccer practices. Steven had the schedule for the first week. She needed to be certain the second week's schedule reached Steven as well. The best assurance of that would be to call the coach. Elizabeth had been selected to play on the premier team. Competition for each of the eighteen spots on the team was fierce, and unexcused absences were frowned upon. Failure to call the coach and tell him a player wouldn't be at practice might mean the player couldn't play in the next game.

Judith removed the wad of papers fixed by a magnet to the refrigerator door. She'd observed the team practices, but hadn't as yet had occasion to talk with the coach.

The work phone rang twice before a man's voice answered.

"Gareth MacCauly."

"Hello . . . this is Elizabeth's mother?"

It was silly. She asked a question instead of making the necessary statement. She got a predicable answer.

"Are you?"

"I'm sorry, really I am. This is Judith Thornton. Elizabeth Thornton's mother."

His voice was smooth, concentrated. "Ah, Mrs. Thornton. I've seen you at the field with Elizabeth. What can I do for you?"

"I wanted to call because I'm leaving town for two weeks. I've . . . my mother's died, and. . . ."

"I'm so sorry to hear that. . . ."

"It's okay, thank you. But I needed to let you know I won't be bringing Elizabeth to the field. Her father will be, and I just want to be sure he gets the schedule for practice next week."

"I mail them to your house, so he should. . . ."

"Well, we're divorced, and he might not get it. Elizabeth's staying with him while I'm away, so if you could be sure. . . ."

"Don't worry, really, I'll get it to her at the field."

"Thank you. I. . . ."

"Is there anything else I can do to help?"

"Oh, no, really, nothing else. If you could just be sure she gets it, that's all I need."

"We have a tournament in two weeks. If you're going to be back by then, let me know. It's a traveling tournament, and we'll be in Orange County for two days. We'd like the whole team to stay up there, and we'll need to know if you'll be there. There's plenty of time. Just give me a call at the number on your team roster. If I'm not there, leave the message on my tape so we can make proper arrangements."

"I'll do that. If I can't get you, can I leave the message with your wife?"

"I'm not married. It's best, really, to call the team manager if you can't reach me. That's Annette. You know Annette."

"I do. I'll call her next week. . . ."

They hung up, the last loose end taken care of. And despite the emotional turmoil surrounding her, something he'd said registered separately from the discussion of schedules. Gareth MacCauly wasn't married.

Judith packed the personal items she wanted in her carry-on bag and threw in the morning newspaper for good measure. In less than twenty-four hours she'd be in Ohio.

3

MARILYN RUSSELL SAT in the front row of the crowded courtroom, looking down at her hands clasped tightly on her lap. The veins on her hands were beginning to show and her fingernails were jagged. She wished she'd taken the time to make her hands look better, although chances were no one here would notice. So far, she'd received little attention from anyone. She'd sat outside Department 8 of the Municipal Court, the arraignment court, for close to an hour waiting for Travis Fuller, her husband's attorney, to arrive. When he hadn't, she'd gone into the courtroom and for almost twenty minutes now sat in the front row, waiting for the judge.

The attorney representing her husband requested she dress nicely, and she'd picked out a black cotton dress with a wide white collar trimmed in thick lace, cleaned her shoes, and secured her chestnut-colored hair firmly at the back of her neck with a white scarf.

She picked nervously at her fingernails and looked around. The courtroom held fifty people, and there were no vacant seats. Some were filled with men and women in suits. Most, she surmised, were attorneys. They pecked away at laptop computers and noisily flipped the pages of court documents. The rest were a mixture of men and women whose purposes in court were a mystery to her. Some, she knew, were defendants, others were family and friends who'd come to lend support.

She sat alone in the front row, on this, only her second visit to a courtroom. The first was for a minor traffic ticket. This morning her visit saw her whole world at stake.

As explained to her, the arraignment court was her husband's first step in the criminal trial process. He would enter his plea. Then the judge would listen to his attorney and the prosecutor discuss what plea he was entering and whether there were grounds to release him on bail. She'd been told by Travis Fuller that the chances of securing bail were pretty good because Russell hadn't ever been arrested before, and he'd lived in the community and in the same house for twelve years. There was reason to be optimistic. Yet Marilyn was uneasy with Fuller. He'd never handled a child molest case before, and from what little she knew about the offense, it was a difficult one to try. Prosecutors didn't give an inch and wanted yards in return for what they did give up in plea and sentencing agreements. So Fuller's optimism frightened her more than it reassured her.

It wasn't just Travis Fuller's lack of experience that caused Marilyn Russell vague discomfort. She would never admit it out loud, but it was the way the man looked and acted, his general impression. He was disheveled two of the three times she'd met with him. She'd given great leeway to the state of his wardrobe as she was certain much of his work must take place in the darkness of the county jail at all hours of the day and night. Still, what a lawyer wore either impressed the jury or it didn't. It either cloaked a person in an air of confidence or it didn't. Wasn't that part of the lecture he'd given *her?*

Through the chaos of the courtroooom, Marilyn spotted Travis Fuller across the aisle, in animated conversation with another attorney. Fuller was wearing a brown corduroy sports jacket and tan pants. At the same moment, it seemed, he spied Marilyn in the front row and walked quickly over to her, his hands outstretched.

"Well, I think I can convince the judge to release Tom," he announced, clasping her hands in his own. His voice was louder than necessary, and Marilyn wasn't sure whether the proclamation was for her or for the people sitting close to her. She managed a weak smile.

"I'm prepared to mortgage the house if I have to, or put the house up as collateral for bail. I've already called the bail bondsman, and he said it could be arranged."

"That's an option. I'll be sure to present it to the judge if we need to. It's done, putting property up as a collateral, but the courts don't like it. They tend to look. . . ."

Their conversation was interrupted as the attention of the courtroom was drawn to the entrance of a group of men through the door at the back corner. All were dressed in baggy gray cotton pants and gray cotton shirts imprinted on the back with large black lettering, "Property of San Diego County Jail." Each man was handcuffed. They shuffled noisily into the jury box and sat, waiting for court to begin.

"Where's Tom?" Marilyn asked nervously, unable to see her husband in the group.

"He'll be the last one brought in. They hold all the child molests 'til last so the other inmates don't hear or see the people charged with those offenses. I specifically asked he not be brought into court until everyone else has been arraigned."

"Why would you want to leave him for last?"

Fuller was hesitant. His face turned pink as he tried to find the right words.

"Well, let's just say inmates can treat people charged with molests pretty badly."

Marilyn's eyes widened and Fuller hastened to add, "But don't worry, the guards watch 'em pretty well."

He was thinking he should be crossing his fingers behind his back. The guards couldn't watch everyone all the time, and there was no question Russell was in trouble if he stayed in jail. Fuller knew it, the prosecutor and court knew it. Child molesters were detested by other inmates and easy marks most of the time. Russell would be isolated to minimize the risks that others might beat or even sexually assault him.

The telephone on the clerk's desk next to the judge's bench buzzed twice and the bailiff snapped to attention, his eyes riveted on the doorway behind the clerk's desk. Two buzzes meant the judge was ready to enter. A moment later, a small woman wearing a black robe stopped at the doorway, entering only when the bailiff called out, "All rise, the Honorable Miriam Peterson presiding." The courtroom bustled with the sound of people rising in unison as she climbed four steps to a large red leather chair. There was another wave of courtroom noise as the deputy yelled, "Be seated," and they sat, shifting into position, ready to respond to their case names and numbers.

The judge, a short, heavy woman with thick curly brown hair framing her face peered over the bench into the courtroom and issued a perfunctory, "Good Morning." She reached for the pile of cases in the center of her bench, and starting at the top, began calling out the defendants' names. The cases were not stacked randomly. The clerk placed the less complicated matters at the top and the more time consuming of them at the bottom, to be heard last.

One by one, as the men's names were called, they were allowed out of the jury box by an armed deputy sheriff and ushered forward with their attorneys. Each was asked how he wished to plead. Some looked at their attorneys and waited for the right nod of the head.

Some requested time to talk with counsel before responding. But in the end, each pleaded not guilty. They all needed time. Time to prepare their cases. Time to bargain with the prosecutor for a good deal, if any deal was in the offing.

Sometimes they didn't know quite what to do and the exasperated judge would help out, once going so far as to tell a procrastinating defendant to "just look at your attorney. If he nods, that means yes. If he shakes his head, that means no."

Had anyone pleaded guilty, there would be a sentencing date set after the plea was taken. With a plea of not guilty, a preliminary hearing date would be set to decide if there was enough evidence to hold the defendant for a felony trial. After that date was set, the court might consider whether the defendant could be released on bail pending the trial.

When the jury box was empty of defendants, the court took a brief recess, giving the bailiff time to bring Russell into the courtroom from the holding cell beneath the courthouse and allowing him and his attorney time to talk before the plea. Fuller sat alone in the box, waiting patiently for him. Then he sat next to him, his hands folded between his knees. He talked and Russell listened, nodding occasionally, but Russell's eyes were on Marilyn.

Throughout the arraignment of the defendants, a single prosecutor sat alone at the desk, responding to each man's case. When Russell entered the courtroom, however, the prosecutor began to pack up, carefully stacking his files in the corner of the desk, then loading them into a large black briefcase on rollers. As he cleared away the last of the files, Aaron Mercer strode into the courtroom and stood beside him. They exchanged a perfunctory greeting and Mercer sat down, waiting for the Russell case to be called.

Russell eyed the new arrival as Fuller explained that his case was being handled by the child abuse unit headed by Mercer. "Nothing unusual. Don't sweat it ... routine," Fuller consoled the suddenly anxious man.

Marilyn, too, had noticed the change in personnel. For her, however, the appearance of Mercer represented a glimmer of hope. He was tall. White-haired. Older than the prosecutor who'd left. More mature, undoubtedly more experienced. This man, who held her life in his hands, was wearing an expensive suit and he wore it elegantly, with nary a wrinkle when he moved. He was the epitome, it seemed to her, of what a man of justice ought to look like. He could have stepped up into the judge's bench and taken her place, so imbued was he with an aura of propriety. His voice evoked the same reassuring feelings. His laughter was smooth and low as he conversed with the younger prosecutor, gentle as he crossed the well of the courtroom, greeting a clearly flattered bailiff by his first name. Everyone, it seemed, reacted as if they were fortunate to be in his presence. The courtroom belonged to him.

He must be, Marilyn thought, above all else, an honorable man.

And where was Fuller while the new arrival worked the courtroom? He sat silently in the box next to Russell, not leaving to greet Mercer. Indeed, neither man ever acknowledged the presence of the other.

When the judge returned, this time without announcement, Mercer retreated to the prosecutor's desk and Russell was led to the defense desk by one of the courtroom deputies. Fuller stood at the podium between the two desks. When Russell was asked what plea he entered, he followed Fuller's advice and said simply, "Not guilty." His voice was soft, barely audible to Marilyn. The new prosecutor did not rise as the judge addressed Russell. However, when the subject turned to whether Russell should be released on bail, Mercer pushed his chair back from the table and rose, listening, expressionless as Fuller made a passionate argument, pointing out Russell's lack of prior criminal offenses, his stable employment, and his ties to the community. When he was through, the judge turned to Mercer.

"I'd like to hear from the People. Mr. Mercer?"

The judge did not need to ask who he was. He must be, Marilyn thought, a man of considerable reputation.

"For the record, Your Honor, Aaron Mercer, deputy district attorney. My concern is that if this man is returned to his home, he might commit the same assault against his daughter."

This man? Might commit the same assault against his daughter? He had it wrong, Marilyn corrected in her own mind. The defendant was not *this man*. He was her husband. Tom Russell. Tom Russell, who had never committed a serious crime in his whole life. Who worked ten-, sometimes eleven-hour days. Who drove his daughter to school every day and stayed home even to take care of the children if they were sick. He was not *this man*.

"It's not possible, Your Honor, that he could commit the same offense again," Fuller interrupted. "Caryn has been in a foster home since the day after the assault. There's no risk letting him return to his house. He's no flight risk."

Mercer was suddenly cold, direct. "Then the question is, Your Honor, is whether this man returns home . . . or his child does."

Russell leaned over and whispered in Fuller's ear as his attorney began to speak.

"Your Honor, I can't agree that my client's a danger to his daughter, but my client informs me that if the court is inclined to return the child to the family home and take her out of foster care, he will withdraw his request for bail. He would rather remain in jail than subject his child to any further trauma." He shook his head dramatically. "I strongly disagree with this, Judge, but I can see his point."

The judge shifted uneasily and looked at Mercer. "I can as well. Mr. Mercer? Your thoughts?"

"Your Honor, I oppose the child being returned. She's been through enough trauma already. I think she needs to be in a safe environment until this criminal matter is resolved."

"But Judge, there's no reason to keep the girl away from her house, her friends. Her mother. I'd remind the court that there's no evidence her mother committed any offense. And there's the consideration of school. She should be going to the same school, if possible."

The judge turned to Mercer.

Up to this point, there was no indication Mercer knew who Marilyn Russell was or whether she was seated anywhere in the courtroom. But he turned and stared at her before addressing the court.

"Marilyn Russell *was* there, Your Honor, in the house, and is required by law to protect her daughter, which she failed to do."

At that moment, Marilyn Russell stopped liking Aaron Mercer, stopped thinking he was going to set things right.

"Mr. Mercer?" the judge continued.

"Yes, Your Honor?"

"I will allow Mr. Russell to withdraw his request for bail if your office states now, on the record, that it will not oppose a request for his daughter's return home. If you aren't prepared to enter into such an agreement, Mr. Russell will have bail set by me now. I'm not the judge who's charged with custody and child dependency matters. But it seems to me I can make the kind of ruling that results in the scenario I've set out. Mr. Fuller?"

"Yes, Your Honor?"

"I'd like to know if my proposal is acceptable to you."

"It is, Judge."

"And you, Mr. Mercer?"

It seemed such a simple choice, yet Mercer was clearly agonizing over the decision. "Can I think about this, Your Honor?"

"It's not a tough choice, Mr. Mercer. If the child must remain in foster care, her father's hardly a threat to her and I'll set bail."

"I'd prefer the defendant remain in jail. It's our office policy to protect the public whenever a case merits it, and this one does."

"Okay, Mr. Russell. Do you withdraw your request for bail at this time?"

Tom Russell nodded as Fuller spoke for him.

"He does, Your Honor, on the condition it may be renewed if the People oppose the request we file in Family Court to return Caryn to the family residence."

"That's acceptable to the court. I'm sure Mr. Mercer will comply. Bail is deemed withdrawn. The preliminary hearing is set for thirty days from today. Is that satisfactory?"

"It is, Judge," Mercer said.

"My client will agree to that," Fuller added.

"Then the clerk will give you the paperwork, Counsel, with the next court date on it. We're in recess until eight-thirty tomorrow morning."

Mercer left the courtroom quickly, without greeting Marilyn, without acknowledging her presence, despite passing within a foot of where she sat. She sensed an insurmountable distance between him and her, a distance as wide as that between the pastel yellow silk of his shirt and the thin worn cotton of her dress.

It was a distance which she knew intuitively could never be bridged. Her first impression of the man had deceived her. He was too far above all of them to see the truth. In Mercer's eyes, Tom was guilty. In the tone of his voice, she knew he would stop at nothing short of convicting him of this awful crime, a crime he did not commit.

Fuller sat talking with Tom in the jury box as a deputy sheriff stood nearby. Marilyn Russell remained seated, standing only as Tom, led out the back door to the holding tank below the courthouse, turned once and managed a weak smile at their small victory.

4

TOM RUSSELL SAT on the bunk bed in the darkened cell. A week ago tonight at about this same time he was at Caryn's school open house, looking at crayon pictures of Hopi Indian dwellings and listening to a teacher with red hair and freckles. How could life change so drastically in seven days? That's what it had been now, just seven days. In seven days life had fallen apart. He tried to concentrate on the important night, the one when Caryn was attacked, tried to remember the events and in what order the events took place. He'd been drinking. He could admit that to himself but not to anyone else, not even Marilyn, or the man defending him in court. He'd been drinking hard liquor. Vodka collinses. That much he could recall. But there were things about that night he couldn't remember. He just couldn't remember. Like how many drinks he'd had, or what time he'd finally gone to bed. Like whether he'd walked into Caryn's bedroom first. He could remember feeling closed in, trapped by the house, the children, his wife. Everything. He'd been feeling sorry for himself and unable to talk to Marilyn about it, and so he'd done what he'd been doing for a long time. He'd had a few drinks. He'd felt angry when he'd started drinking, but then he'd felt nothing. But he wouldn't have hurt Caryn.

Tom Russell raised his hands to cover his face. He couldn't remember doing anything to Caryn. But he couldn't remember *not* doing anything to her, either.

5

IT WAS A bad dream, and Judith knew it even before she forced herself awake in the still blackened bedroom. Her mother was standing next to her at the white-tiled counter facing the kitchen, her voice sad and hollow, her face a terror of darkened cheeks with skin peeling in jagged layers. She'd risen from the dead to deliver a message to Judith. "I miss scrambled eggs the most."

The sound of crashing cars startled Judith awake. She quickly oriented herself and the catastrophe of metal against metal in the soft blue glow of the television screen. She was in a hotel in Canton, Ohio, where she'd fallen asleep watching television. A chase scene from the movie *Die Hard* awakened her. The movie was her mother's favorite. Judith had played the tape for her over and over, watching her stare intently at the action. It was an oddly appropriate touch tonight. Or was it morning? The glowing digits of the clock radio said it was 5:30.

The hotel room air conditioner clicked on, and Judith noticed the room was cold and smelled of cigarettes. She'd arrived the previous evening, and although she'd called to be sure her mother had arrived at the funeral home, she hadn't called her aunt to let her know she was in Canton. Perhaps the relatives wouldn't see this lapse as disrespectful, but the desperate need for privacy and space that it was. She'd wait until 9 o'clock and call when family members started arriving at her aunt's house.

Several minutes passed as Judith lay in bed trying to put into order the events set for the next day. As promised by the funeral home in San Diego, her mother had arrived at the mortuary without a glitch. It was a huge relief, knowing she hadn't taken any unpredictable detours. The ease with which it all had happened surprised her and led her to believe interstate transfers of the dead took place far more often than anyone openly discussed. But she'd never get on a plane again without wondering who else was in the hold below her.

A rosary was scheduled that evening at the funeral home and she expected that a large contingent of friends and family would be in attendance. Sadly, it would be the first time some of them would have seen her mother in more than two years. Such a long time. Her aunt was at least eighty-one now, and Judith worried what effect the sight of her dead sister would have. There were also her three uncles, all in various stages of aging, each with a different level of frailty to contend with.

Fortunately, there were enough children and grandchildren to conduct the necessary activities and make the burial arrangements. One of Judith's cousins, Linda, was a practical nurse who, having a better grasp of the practicalities of death than the rest of the family, had stepped in to assure the local funeral arrangements were complete. There wasn't much for Judith to do except be sure the funeral home had the dress she'd brought for her mother. And the penny. The penny had to be placed under the small pillow at her mother's head. It was one of only two requests Judith had made to Linda when she'd talked with her over the phone. *Be sure Mom looks nice. And be sure the penny is there, at her head.*

Judith gazed at the open closet near the bathroom door where the floral print dress hung next to the black knit suit she'd brought for the funeral tomorrow morning.

Judith pushed away the covers and sat on the edge of the bed. She hated traveling, hated being away from home, and longed for this to be over. Since her mother's death, maybe even before her mother's death, each hour was getting through the next step, and the next day, suspended in a void, being pushed from one emotionless act to another, on cruise control down a road toward the only predictable outcome. Then the ceremonial functions.

Judith walked to the window and pulled the long cord to part the heavy gold brocade curtains. She took a deep breath and a gasp of air and uttered a long "Ohhhhh . . . my . . . God."

The city square, six stories below, was covered with a thick white blanket of snow, and the trees ringing the square, their small decorative white lights still ablaze, were dusted with the white powder. It was not yet morning, but that moment between night and day when the earth is suspended between darkness and light, when anticipation of life overwhelms the darkness of sleep in a surrealistic dream world. And here it glistened in white. In the world below, outside, there was no movement. Not a limb swayed. Not a leaf or piece of paper on the ground moved. There was no traffic, not a sound to suggest any soul in the world had yet awakened, not a movement to suggest anyone except her had yet to witness this ethereal manifestation of nature. This was a strange and wondrous offering, a gift, for her. Some things are profound in their existence alone. The world below was such, and all the more, for when the curtains parted and Judith felt the full impact of what lay below, there was a simultaneous thought of her mother. *It could not have been a coincidence. She did not want it to be coincidence.*

Never a person of the church, Judith felt something profound. Not the hand of God. Not an angel's whispering. It was a deep and comforting sweetness of pain turned inside out, near joy but not joyous. The thought was not hers, because she would not on her own have felt its message. It came from somewhere else. *Everything's going to be all right.* And the thought and the beauty accompanying it made her want to cry, it seared her heart too deeply and so thoroughly. But she hovered instead on the brink, holding the sight and the feeling that some important message, so simple, had overwhelmed her, and for several minutes she exalted in it, unwilling to move.

Then Judith strained to look downward left and right out the window. She'd visited this square hundreds of times as a child. It was just as she remembered it.

She turned from the window and looked toward the closet where the floral dress hung, now sadly out of season. She'd brought a coat because cold weather had been predicted, but she'd neglected to bring boots or clothing suitable for snow. Yet what did the lack of proper clothing matter? If she got wet or cold, her room was minutes from it. It was hours before she'd leave for either the funeral home or her aunt's house. Judith grabbed the velour sweatsuit from her open suitcase, her only thought that the last time she'd worn it, she'd humiliated Aaron Mercer in the grocery store. She grabbed the caramel-colored coat her mother had given her for Christmas six years earlier. Less than a minute later, she was in the empty hotel hallway, passing doors behind which people still slept and before which the morning newspapers still waited to be read.

In the square below, a trail of footprints led from the hotel past a large man-sized statue of an archangel, to the black wrought-iron bench where Judith sat clutching the coat to her chest. In her haste she'd left without gloves, and her fingers froze as she rubbed her hand into the dense layer of snow on the bench. She closed her eyes. *It was the morning after Christmas. The last Christmas she lived in Ohio. Her mother had bundled her for the snow. So heavily*

*padded with clothing was she that it was difficult
to move and impossible to play in the cold. Her
mittens noisily crushed the white snow and she
pushed it into small piles, a mock snowman. At last
she'd given up and returned to the house, hot and
sticky, and crying to her mother that she felt so
very cheated. The snow was for playing, and even
in the midst of it she couldn't touch it. Her mother
smiled and told her there would be other times to
play in the snow. But she could remember no other
time.*

Judith reached out and grabbed a handful
of the cold ice. Then another. Until she possessed a large snowball which she aimed, then
threw somewhat haphazardly at the archangel
statue, hitting it squarely in the face, leaving a
mustache of white across its upper lip. She
formed yet another and aimed it as well, this
time at the birdbath at the angel's feet. The
throwing continued until her hands were frozen to numbness and finally buried in the coat
pockets.

This soft white in the midst of darkness, this
sign of gentleness in a torrent of pain, this
benediction in the face of remorse, was hers,
and she sat alone on the bench, cold yet content, until the square began to fill with people
and the thought of scrambled eggs and toast
lured her inside.

Judith recognized the huge white house as
soon as the cab rounded the corner of Main
Street. Seven or eight cars were parked outside, portending a large gathering inside. As
she walked through the front door, a stream

of people moved from the kitchen into the foyer where she stood, pulling the coat from her shoulders.

"It's Judith! She's here!"

Cries of welcome and announcement from adjoining rooms greeted Judith's entrance. And she yelled back, greetings of joy and surprise at faces she hadn't seen since her childhood. No one was crying. There were smiles and warm hugs. What did she expect, black bunting around the doors? Loud weeping, audible from the street? There was none of that, and it slightly surprised and relieved her. Her Aunt Martha stepped next to her and guided her into the kitchen and a waiting cup of coffee. She had shrunk in her old age, or Judith remembered her much taller than she was in fact.

The next hour was filled with talk of home, of her mother's last year, and of Elizabeth. How tall she was, how she was doing in school, and questions about why she hadn't brought her back to the funeral. In truth, she could have come. The fears Judith had concerning the morose nature of the visit had been dispelled. But it was just as well. And the explanations were readily accepted.

Eventually talk turned to her, to Judith. How she was doing. How her hair looked and how sophisticated she appeared. Everyone was duly impressed with her job title and the importance of her work. As the conversation wound down, the phone in the kitchen rang and her aunt rose to an arthritic bend at the waist and hobbled to answer the call. The room hushed as her aunt's face turned ashen and a cousin, Harry, took the receiver from her and resumed the conversation.

"Why scare her like that?" he half-yelled into the mouthpiece, shaking his head in disgust as the poor woman seemed to shrink against him. "Okay, okay. Of course she'll look fine! Tell her that yourself and watch, for Christ's sake, what you're saying!" He handed the receiver back to Judith's aunt and took a chair next to Judith at the table as someone poured her another cup of coffee.

"What happened?" Judith asked.

"That damned Carol." Carol was the nurse making the arrangements for the funeral. "She went and told her your mother's body looks horrible but they're working on her. Especially on her hair. Can you imagine saying anything like that to her?"

Judith felt her own face grow cold and imagined it was as white as her aunt's.

Suddenly remembering to whom he was speaking, Harry apologized loudly. "Oh, God, I'm sorry!" he wailed, as his eyes filled with tears. "I shouldn't be telling *you* that."

He was so stricken by his faux pas that Judith found herself comforting the man. "It's okay." Judith whispered. "Really. It's okay. I don't imagine she's going to look super. It's been a few days and Mom's been traveling, you know." The whole discussion was beginning to strike her as extremely funny, as if her mother were suffering from a severe case of jet lag. She welcomed the exclamation from one of the relatives milling about behind her.

"The casket has to be kept shut at the rosary tonight, or poor Aunt Martha's going to wilt on us."

A quick and informal consensus taken was that the casket lid be kept shut. Judith herself, seeing the whiteness of her aunt's face and feeling her own nightmares might come true when she gazed on her mother the next time, agreed.

The casket would remain closed.

The rosary at Bougher Brothers Mortuary was set for 7 o'clock. Judith had stayed at the house visiting most of the day, then delivered the floral dress to the mortuary. At 6:30 she arrived at the door of the small chapel where her mother lay in the pink casket she'd selected in San Diego days earlier. The director of the funeral home solemnly greeted her with an ever-so-slight bow and took her elbow in his hand, preparing to guide her inside. But he stopped in his tracks and looked sideways at Judith when she announced she was going in to visit with her mother but afterward the casket lid must be closed for the rosary.

"But . . ." he stammered, his eyes wide. She knew what he was thinking. *So much work has gone into making her look presentable . . .*

Judith was adamant. The relatives, some of them very elderly, had to be spared the grief of seeing her. She was feeling much in control of the situation as he nodded his consent and opened the chapel door for her. At the far wall, the pink casket stood, the top half of it open, revealing her mother's body from head to waist. And her mother—it was the moment her nightmares warned her about. But surprise! There was no skeletal face. No grotesque apparition. Her mother looked . . . there was only one word to describe her . . . *beautiful*. Her face was full and gently colored, her hair combed into a short style she'd worn a decade earlier, her hands folded neatly at her chest. The pinks and blue of the floral dress were delicate against the flower arrangements of pastel pink, yellow, and white roses covering the bottom half of the casket. This was nothing to hide. Indeed, this view of her mother *needed* to be seen, *needed* to be the last one her relatives and friends saw before she disappeared from the face of the earth forever.

Judith knelt at the step next to her mother's coffin. She reached out and rested the tips of her fingers on her mother's cheek, finding it cold, stiff, and hard. The life was gone from her. Her condition, this shell, proof enough that there used to be something else in there. Life, whatever life is, was in there once, and now it had to be somewhere else. Judith stroked her mother's smooth, stiff forehead and reflected on the human touch. Before tonight, before touching her mother's face, she'd taken the feeling of life for granted.

Judith sat next to the casket until the doors at the back of the chapel opened and the funeral director closed them behind him. He hurried toward Judith, wringing his hands.

"Mrs. Thornton," he said, his voice quavering, "there's a very large crowd gathered and I don't think we should, or can, keep them waiting. There's a good hundred people wandering around."

"One hundred?" Judith questioned.

"Yes, a good hundred. Can't we please let them in?"

"Of course."

"Should I still close the casket?"

Judith looked at her mother, beautiful in death, not the horrible cadaver her poor aunt was terrified at seeing.

"I guess so, yes."

The director shook his head in apparent disbelief, and he and Judith closed the coffin, Judith watching her mother's beautifully coifed head disappear into the darkness of the pink casket.

The funeral director moved one of the larger flower sprays of white roses onto the center of the casket and then hurried toward the doors, opening them to a large group of people who walked to the rows of chairs and sat down. Judith stood by the casket and watched them carefully. She quickly observed a thread of communication, a wave of disappointment, spreading through the room. It started slowly at first. They stared at the closed casket. Then they began to stare at each other. Several shrugged to others across the room.

They had come to see her mother. It was as if they'd sold tickets and canceled the show. It was, after all, a "showing."

Judith smiled and walked to Harry, who was seated in the center of the front row. He'd brought a small pile of old family pictures of her mother and was passing them down the aisle. They were being eagerly grabbed by the disappointed guests.

"Look how beautiful your mother was!"

"She was always the prettiest one in the family, Judith."

Judith agreed with each comment, but when the opportunity presented itself, turned to her picture-passing relative.

"Harry, I think we should open the casket."

"But your aunt. . . ."

"Mom looks wonderful, beautiful. We *have* to open it. All these people came to see her, Harry. And I think it would do the relatives all good to see Mom for the last time looking so pretty."

He turned and looked over his shoulder at the room, now at standing room only capacity.

"Okay, but. . . ."

"Don't worry, I'll be responsible for Aunt Martha. I promise, Mom looks wonderful."

Judith wiggled her index finger at the funeral director, calling him from the corner to where he'd sullenly retreated. He was most anxious to comply with this new request, and smiling, with a full audience looking on, he and Judith walked ceremoniously together to the coffin and lifted the lid.

It was quite the dramatic moment. With a flourish, her mother suddenly reappeared and an approving murmur spread through the room. Heads nodded and faces lit with smiles. She looked beautiful, and Judith realized this was what they all had come to see, needed to see. All the aunts and uncles. All the old school friends of her mother and the families that knew her when she was little. They needed to see her looking like this. They needed to see death beautiful. Oh, how her mother would have loved this entrance. Would have loved how she looked.

Within minutes, people were circulating, greeting each other with warm hugs and re- membrances. There were familiar gazes at her mother and signs of the cross made by people who approached the coffin to kneel and offer a prayer.

Judith stood at the head of the casket greet- ing people. Some of them she knew, others were introduced. They came from all walks of life. A distant cousin who was an elementary school teacher, an old boyfriend from child- hood. The neighbors around the corner. Even the member of the city council in whose dis- trict the family lived. It went on and on for two hours until the last of the guests either said good-bye or that they would see her at the burial tomorrow morning.

At the end, when the last person left, the director approached and she knew the time had come to say good-bye again.

"Can I be alone with her for a few minutes?"

Now happy, his rosary evening an unmiti- gated success, he nodded approvingly.

"Just call me when you need me."

Judith knelt at her mother's head and stared at her. She ran her hand again over her cheeks. As she stood, she broke a small flower, one of the filler flowers, a delicate purple, from the floral spray on the coffin at her mother's feet and pushed it between the fingers of her mother's hands. She reached gently under the pink satin pillow her head rested on. The small cold metal object moved freely under Judith's fingers. The penny was there, where it was supposed to be.

She touched the side of her mother's cheek again and reached for the rim of the casket top. She didn't want to close it, yet she wanted no one else to close it. She had the sense to realize the significance of the moment. As it lowered, Judith watched her mother's face until it once again disappeared behind the pink steel. She pressed her own cheek against the coffin top.

Judith awakened the following morning to the distant sound of the wind. Where the previous day a pristine scene awaited her in the square below her window, today the snow flurries swirled in vicious semi-circles as people ran around and through them for cover.

The drive to the funeral home was slow as Harry's car fishtailed its way up one street and down another, finally coming to a rest at the front door. Inside, members of the family had already gathered, bundled in dark coats and thick wool scarves. They quickly piled into the waiting black limousines behind the hearse carrying the casket and the entire entourage wound its way slowly to the church where the family had worshipped and married and held funeral services for several decades.

The church service lasted thirty minutes. Although the priest was familiar with the family, he hadn't known Judith's mother personally. He did his best to sound familiar with her, but his words had little meaning to Judith except that they served to distract her from the thick and bothersome smell of incense wafting in her direction. There was another migration to the limousines as the casket holding her mother was loaded again into the hearse and the entire group headed for the cemetery and small chapel there.

By the time Judith and the family reached the chapel and the last blessing was held at the casket's side, the temperature had plummeted to three degrees. The snow stopped, but the bitter cold reduced Judith's aunt to immobility. The concern shifted imperceptibly from the dead to the safety and health of the elder family members. Should they walk up the steep hill to the grave? Was it starting to snow? Harry announced they would not "go graveside." His pronouncement was greeted with fragile smiles and only light protest. Any resistance or guilt felt was upstaged by the priest, who, having gone to survey the grave sight, suddenly appeared at the chapel door and somberly informed all in attendance that the ground had been too frozen to finish digging the grave. They couldn't bury Judith's mother this morning even if they'd been inclined to. Their fate for the morning sealed, the burial was officially called off. It would not go on until the bitter cold relented enough to dig.

Judith and her family were forced once again to say good-bye, but this time at the chapel, with a promise the casket would be guarded and the pallbearers, six of the male family members, would see the burial took place with proper dignity.

Judith's flight home was scheduled for the following evening. If the freeze lasted beyond the next morning, she might not see her mother buried. For reasons unexplainable, Judith felt the funeral was over for her, the act of seeing her mother placed in the ground immaterial. She knew she *should* want to see that final act, it was her *obligation* to see this through to the very last, but in a fundamental way, it didn't matter.

Judith didn't see the funeral. The freeze lasted three more days, long after Judith's flight lifted off for home. And as she watched the lights of Canton disappear below her, it occurred to Judith that at every step of the way, fate or some higher force had spared her the worst sights of death.

The airport shuttle van dropped Judith at her front door shortly after 9 P.M. The house was cold and dark. It was the silence, though, that was particularly noticeable; the absence of all other life was different. The suitcases near the doorway could remain there until morning. It was too late to unpack. She grabbed four newspapers from the top of the stack and threw herself onto the living room couch, leafing through the papers quickly.

The last of the newspapers caused her to sit upright, then rise and walk to the kitchen, where the light was brighter. The paper was almost a week old, but the headline of the article on the front page in the local section was of immediate interest. "Man Accused of Assault on Daughter." Her fingers traced the single-column story. Thomas Russell had been charged with assaulting his daughter. She read on. The prosecutor, Aaron Mercer, had called a press conference afterward to announce a new get-tough policy of the District Attorney's Office on sexual predators.

Had they found some new item of evidence while she was away?

She glanced at the clock. It was too late to call Larry Farrell.

It was Mercer. He'd offered to help. Help, all right. He'd gotten what he wanted. But there was some explaining to do. She'd planned on taking the next day off work, but Elizabeth wouldn't be home until evening tomorrow, and without some explanation, there was no way she'd allow this to go unanswered.

6

AARON MERCER CONSIDERED discretion, the power of choice, to be the most powerful tool in the justice system. It's the police officer who decides he's going to give you a warning instead of a traffic ticket; the judge who puts the defendant on probation instead of sentencing him to state prison; the prosecutor who has in his hand a file and has to decide what to do with the case in the file.

Should he file charges against the defendant or not?

Should he drop the charges if someone else has filed them?

Is there enough evidence to charge the defendant?

Even if there's enough evidence to charge the defendant, is it the right time to charge him?

It was all there in the application of discretion, the heart and breath of the justice system, its humanity. And its power. Aaron Mercer, above all, loved power: the raw power of his discretion.

The blue pen was poised in his hands, suspended above the thin black line at the bottom of the document. With a stroke of pen, Thomas Russell would officially be a criminal defendant. Mercer set the pen on his desk next to the document, withholding his signature and thus the sweeping power of the law. Not yet.

He needed to think on this a bit more. It really wasn't a slam-dunk call, even for him, and if he made the decision to prosecute, he'd be throwing the whole of his energy into it.

Mercer stood and walked to the large street map of San Diego fixed by small nails to the wall behind his desk. His eyes swept the entirety of it and settled at last on the Point Loma area, at the end of Rosecrans Boulevard. He'd spent some time running the crime stats for a three-mile radius around the Russell home and he'd come up with some information worth noting.

In his hand were three red-topped stickpins, pressed perilously against the skin. One he stuck on the corner of Desmond Avenue and Tulip Street. The second he inserted into the corner of Truax and Hawthorne Streets, just five blocks south of the first pin. It took a moment for him to find the precise location for the third pin, but he located the corner of Dale and Croft Streets and pushed the head of the pin into the paper.

Mercer cocked his head slightly to the right. The Russell home was located almost central to the first two pins, perhaps two miles from one and a mile from the other. Alone, the location of the pins was an interesting coincidence. Each represented a place, a home, where a sexual assault crime similar to the crime committed against Caryn Russell had taken place. Both involved children, ages seven and nine. One involved an assailant who'd carried the girl outside. Both of them had occurred after Tom Russell's arrest, so he was not a suspect in either of them. In one of the two other cases, involving the seven-year-old, a suspect had been arrested. That man, an acquaintance of the girl who'd been assaulted, confessed to that crime and that of the nine-year-old. And as it turned out, he was a friend of one of the victims' families. He was plenty remorseful and wanted to plead guilty to both offenses. His cases would never see the light of day. There was an interesting coincidence of two or three: in his mind, nothing more than an interesting footnote, of no legal consequence.

Oh, to be sure, some clever defense attorney might claim there was a similarity that required the facts of those cases be used in the Russell case as a defense, or to show he didn't commit the crime he was charged with, that someone else, the someone else committing *these* crimes, had also committed the atrocity against Caryn. Some might say it would show Tom Russell was an innocent man, an honorable man. But no good prosecutor would allow such evidence in, and no judge worth his salt would admit such evidence over a prosecutor's objection. They'd tried it against Mercer before. Some serial robber suddenly claims in court that the similar crimes in the east part of the city are by the same person who committed the crimes he was charged with in the west part of the city. In his experience, good trial judges always denied defense requests to admit such evidence of similar crimes. There was nothing wrong with those rulings, either.

The law was clearly on his side. A trial had to be kept to the facts, only the facts of the case then in court. Or any other, lest a whole hornet's nest of other evidence come in. The law doesn't like to open a case to the outer world of such mischief. You'd end up trying one or more of the other cases.

So as intriguing as it might be, none of the red pins was relevant to Russell's case—had anything to do with what *Russell* had done the night Caryn was assaulted.

But it was interesting, he had to admit that.

Mercer left the red pins where he'd stuck them and sat down again at his desk, lifting the pen to his mouth, gently biting the top. Before him sat the files from the other cases. He opened one, then the other, looking into the eyes of the suspect's booking photo—looking into the pockmarked face of Arthur Whaley, a two-time loser from Colorado, who, unless he had a damned good attorney, was headed to prison, probably for life.

Mercer placed the Whaley files in the outbox to be returned to the trial deputy who'd be taking his place in a month, after the probation report was prepared. Then he signed his name on the bottom line of the Russell charging document and placed it in the outbox for filing in the morning.

* * *

Judith Thornton had forgotten it was the first day of the month, and every welfare and social security check in the city seemed to be in the bank line ahead of her. She'd come to cash a check and had encountered a line of perhaps fifteen people. If she were lucky, it would take twenty minutes to get through to a teller. She wasn't used to waiting in lines like this. Her checks were automatically deposited and her bills were automatically paid from the deposit. If she made a mistake in her account, she got a courtesy call from the bank and transferred funds from her savings to cover the mistake. She glanced at the large wood-framed clock on the wall to her right. It was one o'clock, and she needed to be back in her office at 1:30. The thought crossed her mind that she should leave and come back later, when the wait wouldn't be so bad. But there was something about standing there in line that invigorated her, causing her to stay the course.

The woman dressed in black stretch pants and black sweatshirt clutched a paper in her hand. The paper was a check, stiff and pale green, obviously government issued. She was talking to the man next to her—at least, that's what Judith Thornton thought, until the man turned casually and stepped away from the line in an obvious attempt to disassociate himself from the woman. The man's attempts did not dissuade the lady. Although not really addressing him, she tenaciously directed her conversation toward the man, periodically beginning her sentences with, "Excuse me." Yet she clearly was not talking to him and he clearly was ignoring her. It took a moment for Judith to realize the woman was actually talking to God. Telling how she prayed every night. How she was determined to help the black children of the world. A few in the long line stared relentlessly. Most people smiled benignly and tried to pretend the woman was talking to the man. All the pieces of the woman's conversation, the phrases, the sentences, made sense. But the whole was gibberish.

Then, as the woman neared the front of the line, her conversation came to a halt. When it was her turn and the teller called out, "Next, please," she walked to the bank window and carried on a perfectly normal conversation with the teller. Judith watched her fill out the deposit slip, ask for sixty dollars in return, and carefully place the receipt for the transaction in her wallet. The two discussed the beautiful weather and the long bank line and did so in a calm, even voice. There was another call for "Next, please," and Judith approached the teller window, deposited her check, and turned to walk away. The woman spouting gibberish and insanity had disappeared.

There were people from all levels of the city. The attorneys—she recognized one of them. Casually dressed women and men with knapsacks and suntans, ready to do the sightseeing for the day. Tourists. And then there were the street people. Odorous with alcohol on the breath or the stink of uncleanliness, the people in line around them breathing shallowly and stepping back safe distances.

Dressed haphazardly in the layers of their entire wardrobe, or sparsely, even with pants down around the hips. The dirty, waiting with their social security checks clutched in their hands. People around one of them were breathing shallowly. Periodically, there came a murmur under his breath.

PART TWO

PROTOCOL

7

EVEN BEFORE JUDITH poured her first cup of coffee, Mercer was knocking at her office door, gushing with condolences in decibels slightly above normal, sufficient to be heard in the hallway and in the next office. He was sincere, to be sure, but nothing seemed to exist for him at a purely emotional level. Everything had an overlayer of self-interest. Even this. With preliminaries past them, Mercer, office master calendar in hand, sought to bring Judith up to date on the current calendar of cases. One by one, he summarized the more notable events—all, that is, except the Russell case.

Slightly more than a week had passed since her mother's death, and although Judith hadn't any file to follow, that would have placed Thomas Russell at about the ten-day post-arraignment time limit. From the time he'd pleaded not guilty at his arraignment, Russell had ten days to wait for his preliminary hearing, a pretty short period of time.

Everything about the prosecution of Tom

Russell bothered her, including the fact that the case had been stolen from her by Mercer.

"I understand Thomas Russell's still charged in the case against his daughter?" She said it as a question. She meant it as an accusation. Mercer wasn't bothered in the least.

"He is . . . it's a most strong case, Judith."

"It got stronger after I left?"

"Well, of course, it was strong from the outset . . . but we did disagree on that."

There was nothing for Judith to say or do. The case was no longer hers. As adamant as she'd felt the night before, as noble as she felt her position was on the charges, protocol dictated she refrain from pursuing the matter unless Mercer allowed it to be pursued, and he wasn't about to do that. Indeed, he moved the topic of conversation quickly from Russell to the more mundane, in the process succeeding in alienating Judith even more.

"There's a new coffee dispenser in since you left, Judith. You've got your own, but I'd bet this one's twice as fast. It's in the lounge. You ought to try it."

He turned to leave.

"It's good to have you back again."

She ignored the pleasantry.

"Who's representing Russell in the case?"

"Travis Fuller."

"Teflon Travis Fuller?"

As he left her office, Mercer smiled. "The same." Travis Fuller was known as "Teflon" among the prosecutors. it wasn't a nickname he cultivated, but rather was whispered behind his back, in offices where he wasn't present. The term referred to his suits, usually brown polyester.

Judith held her breath. Fuller was no match for Mercer. Aaron would rip him to shreds, and if Russell was an innocent man, she couldn't think of a worse scenario. It wasn't so much the facts of the case and presentation of the case skill that bothered her. It was the out-maneuvering that was certainly going to take place. Teflon was mediocre. Someone who tried mostly drunk driving cases didn't belong in front of a jury on a heavy felony matter with Aaron Mercer. But for the moment there was nothing she could do. Or almost nothing. Judith reached for her phone and pressed four numbers. A woman's voice answered at the other end. Judith was direct.

"Andrea? Can you find the transcript Aaron Mercer had you read a couple of weeks ago? I'd like to take a look at it. And, Andrea? Can you keep this under your hat for now?"

The conference room at the District Attorney's Office was impressive. The oval table was new and the soft burgundy leather chairs showed no signs of wear. The wall decor was a bit stark, but the feeling of public austerity needed to be maintained.

It still placed defense counsel at a psychological disadvantage. Mercer allowed counsel to be shown into the room, only to have him wait, alone, for ten minutes. Fuller busied himself with his files and tried to think of the best approach. Mercer was a formidable opponent. He was also a very busy man. Perhaps a play on his time and resources might force a plea that was advantageous. If that didn't work, he'd appeal to his sense of family, his sense that families should, wherever possible, be re-unified. And he waited. And waited. Twenty minutes after he first sat down, Fuller rose and peeked out into the hallway. The secretary who'd ushered him into the conference room was nowhere to be seen. He ventured outside, now slightly angry at what was a clear rebuff.

He confronted the first secretary he saw. "I had an appointment with Mr. Mercer almost a half hour ago and I've been waiting for him in the conference room."

The secretary rose and hurried off into the direction of a series of offices, one of which was surely Mercer's. "I'll check and be right back," she promised.

"Travis, I'm so sorry!" Mercer bustled into the conference room. "I was all set to meet and I got a long-distance call, an emergency from a judge down in Texas. I apologize." He sat down across from Fuller and began leafing through the thick file he'd brought with him. "Let's see, Thomas ... Russell. Ah, yes. The child molest."

"Alleged child molest," Fuller corrected.

"Yes, alleged, of course."

"Aaron, we're set for the prelim next week. I'm curious what's on the table at this point."

"He pleads to the top charge."

"Rape?"

"Rape. And we dismiss the remaining molest counts."

"That'll net him. . . ." He paused and Mercer filled in the rest.

". . . Three, six or eight years. Eight years max. I'd settle for the midterm six years."

"He won't go for it."

"That's his prerogative."

"The evidence is just as weak as it was two weeks ago, Aaron, unless you've got some information I don't have."

"I think it's just as strong. And the DA's not budging on this one."

Fuller was smart enough to realize the political ramifications of the case. He'd been around long enough to remember the sex case scandal following Larry Farrell into the current election battle.

"And after the prelim?"

"Well, Travis, you know if I have to put Caryn on the stand, there's no deal after the prelim."

That was standard procedure. If the victim in a child molest case had to go through the trauma of taking the stand to testify, any plea offers were off following the testimony.

"It's a hard position, Aaron."

"It's meant to be a hard position. The man assaulted a child."

"I'll need all the reports you've got . . . including any forensics."

"I can give you more time if you'd like to waive the ten-day rule . . . take this out to say, sixty days?"

"I can't. I've got a vacation coming up in two weeks. I'd like to have this matter wrapped up by then."

Mercer was baiting him now. "We don't have many reports back yet, just the preliminaries on the psychological reports. Arrest reports, too, are here for you. Why don't I give the file to my secretary and have her photocopy the file reports for you right now?"

Mercer rose and walked toward the door.

"You won't change your mind about that rape charge?"

He answered without turning back. "Can't do that, Travis."

Ten minutes later Fuller had copies of the reports from the file and headed toward the jail to tell Russell the bad news. He'd have to enter a plea of guilty to raping his daughter, and if he didn't enter that plea by the preliminary hearing, he'd get no plea at all afterward.

Thomas Russell sat motionless in his cell at the end of the hall, waiting for his attorney to arrive. This was the day Fuller promised to explain the preliminary hearing. Fuller usually visited early in the morning, before the second calendar call of the day. This morning, however, he was late. Russell wanted to know his options. Wanted to go home if he could. But the bottom line was he refused to say he did it.

At last the jail guard announced Fuller's arrival. When he came into the waiting area, Russell was seated at the visitor's desk. Fuller was distressed, but not so distressed that he himself failed to notice the decline in the appearance of Russell. The man's brown hair was an uncombed mass of curls. Under his eyes, dark circles evidenced the lack of sleep.

"You didn't shave today?" Fuller asked, as Russell took a seat opposite him.

"Naw, not yet. I will, maybe later. So what did you find out about my case? Are they going to let me go?"

"Jesus Christ, man, no! They aren't going to let you go. They're not even going to let you have a decent plea bargain. Here's the deal: the DA's being a hard-ass. It's because they have a child molest case. They have a public image to uphold here. In the molest cases they'll let you plead to one charge, usually the most serious one, before the preliminary hearing. After that they won't allow you to plead to anything but the entire complaint."

"What's that mean for me?"

"It means that before the prelim they'll let you plead to the rape charge. After the preliminary hearing, you have to plead to all three charges. No deals."

"What kind of plea offer is that?" a bewildered Russell whispered.

"Not much of a plea at all."

Russell was silent for a moment before asking, "Then what do I do?"

"It's a tough choice. If you go through the preliminary hearing, they'll put Caryn on the witness stand. She'll have to answer some pretty tough questions with you sitting right in front of her. It won't be easy for her."

"If, if I did plead guilty to the, the rape charge, what would my sentence be?"

"They'll take the midterm option at six years."

Russell's face turned white. "Six years? In a place like this?"

"No, in a worse place than this."

"There's no place on earth worse than this."

"Think on it, Tom. I know you say you didn't do it."

"I didn't!" Russell interrupted. "I didn't rape my own kid."

"I believe you. But what I think doesn't count. This is all going to come down to expediency. Do you want to put her through trial and then face the possibility you'll be spending the rest of your adult life in a state prison? Just promise me you'll think on it."

"I will. I'll think on it, but can't say I did something I really didn't do."

Fuller stood and walked to Russell's side.

"Tom, I don't usually ask my clients whether they committed the crimes they're charged with. Everyone's entitled to a defense. But I've never handled a case this serious before. If you're convicted of all these sex crimes, you're going away for a very long time. So I'm going to ask you point-blank, and I want you to answer me honestly." There was a pause. "Did you do it?

Russell looked up at him. "I couldn't have done those things to Caryn."

Fuller searched the man's face. The answer was ambiguous, but he didn't pursue it.

"Okay, think on it, though. Just think on it. And Tom, I want to level with you on this, too. I can take this through the prelim and any plea, if there is one. But the trial would be beyond anything I've ever done, from a forensic standpoint. I mean, the tests they have to see if you're the perpetrator are technical. Beyond me. You might need someone with more experience."

"Mr. Fuller?"

"Uh huh?"

"Is there a chance the DA will change his mind?"

"None. None whatsoever."

8

JUDITH LOOKED OUT over the soccer field, trying unsuccessfully to determine where Elizabeth was practicing. She didn't see her daughter, but a woman she recognized as one of the parents approached, sitting next to her on the bleachers. In the course of casual conversation, the subject turned to the dwindling numbers of girls coming to the weekday practices and the coach's not too subtle phone calls to remind the players they were expected to be at all practices unless excused. And then came a question Judith hadn't been expecting.

"Did you hear about Annette?"

Judith's first reaction was to ask, "Annette who?"

"Annette. The woman who visits with you out here all the time."

Judith knew immediately. It was her good friend who'd first persuaded her to have Elizabeth try out for the soccer team.

"Have I heard what?"

"She's really sick."

"Flu?"

"Oh, God, no. Cancer. Ovarian. It's pretty bad."

Judith caught her breath, but didn't respond.

"She's a good friend of yours, isn't she, Judith?"

"Yes. But I didn't know anything about her being so sick."

"No one did. She didn't, either. I gather she'd had symptoms but didn't do anything about them. I don't know much about that kind of cancer, but I know enough about it to hope it hasn't spread to any other organs, like the liver. She's not in the hospital. They sent her home. I don't know what that means, but it can't be good. . . ." The barrage of information was now unnecessary, and it drifted away. Judith was having trouble processing the information. She knew Annette, knew her well. Why hadn't anyone called her to tell her? Judith interrupted the dialogue still pouring from the woman.

"I'll give her a call right away." Judith looked out over the field. "Her daughter's here. Has she been getting to the field okay for practices and games?"

The woman's focus shifted. "There hasn't been much problem there. Annette's sister's been in from Denver for the last few weeks, and things, at least here, seem to be under control."

As the girls began moving toward the bleachers, Judith rose and walked to Annette's daughter. Standing next to her, she put her hand gently on the girl's shoulder.

"Are you doing all right?" The girl nodded. "Tell your mom I'll call her tonight."

Judith watched her walk off toward the parking lot. Then she turned to the man standing at the equipment bag. It was a coach she recognized, and when he said hello, she recognized his voice.

"Annette's a good friend of mine. Can you let me know if there's anything I can do to help out here at the field with her daughter? If she needs a ride home, anything?"

"That's kind of you. It's been no trouble so far. She's getting to practices and hasn't missed a game. But we'll let you know if anything's needed."

Then he walked over to her. "I think we talked on the phone just before you left for your mother's funeral. I'm Gareth MacCauly. I was sorry to hear about your mother's death."

"Thank you. She'd been sick for a long time. But about Annette, she's a good friend. If there's anything. . . ."

He continued the conversation, but now began walking toward the bright orange cones that had marked the ends of the practice field. "Not so far. But we have this tournament coming up next month in Orange County." He took several more steps away from her and she was starting to have trouble hearing what he was saying. But she didn't want to chase him across the field. She assumed he was letting her know Annette might need some help getting her daughter ready for the next tournament.

"I'll check with you later?" Judith yelled back. It was a half-question. More an attempt to end the conversation. Elizabeth by this time was at the car waiting for Judith to open the trunk.

The dinner dishes were in the dishwasher and Elizabeth's homework was done. Judith was looking for something to do. Something to keep her from making the call she'd dreaded making all day. She wanted to talk to Annette. Wanted to find out what medicines she was taking, what doctors she had, whether she needed anything. It was odd, then, that she was having such trouble calling her. She forced herself over to the desk phone and dialed. The voice at the other end wasn't familiar. It was Annette's sister, Ellen. Judith introduced herself. Annette was sleeping, but Ellen knew at once who Judith was.

"She's been asking me to call you, Judith. I think she wants to talk to you."

Here the woman broke down and Judith could hear the stifled sobs. "She has some business that she needs taken care of, legal business."

"Can I help right now?"

"Not really. I think she needs to talk to you here at the house."

"I'll come over this weekend, if you'd like."

"I think you should come sooner. That is, if it's convenient for you. She's on a ventilator. One of those ones you roll along with you. It's got her medication attached to it so she can. . . ." The woman took a deep breath and paused a moment. "So she can medicate herself whenever the pain's too great. We don't know how long she's going to be stable like this. She's in bed most of the day. It's a real effort for her to get up. It's only going to get worse. There's, there's not much more they can do for her because we found out . . . just today . . . that it's spread to her liver. I suspect you know how bad that is."

"I know it's . . . I'm so sorry."

"She'd like to see you, Judith. I think she needs to see you."

"How's tomorrow evening?"

"About seven o'clock?"

"That's perfect. Elizabeth will have a sitter. . . ."

"No, please bring her. I think Annette would love to see her again, and the girls can visit. Please bring her."

"I'll do that, then. Tomorrow night at seven."

"I'm sorry, Marilyn, but I don't like him."

"You've only met him once, Linda. Don't make a snap decision just yet."

Linda Ramert had been trying to stay as objective as she could about her brother-in-law's legal problems. An office manager for a small law firm, she'd solicited opinions from co-workers and had opinions thrust on her. In the end, after several months of following the investigation and first trial steps of Tom Russell, she'd concluded he needed another attorney.

"I've listened to him long enough to understand he's not good enough to handle this case. He's said so himself. He's a drunk driving attorney. He's never represented anyone who's been in such serious trouble."

"He's been kind to us, Linda. I don't know where we. . . ."

She put her hand on her sister's shoulder. "I'm sorry, Marilyn. Travis Fuller just doesn't strike me as the kind of attorney who ought to be representing a defendant in as serious a case as Tom's."

"I still trust him."

Linda was losing patience. "Jesus Christ, Marilyn! Look around you! Your daughter's being pulled apart. One day she loves her father and defends him. The next day, after all that questioning, she's too confused to know whether or not it was her father who raped her! Do you know what's going to happen if they put that little girl on the stand at the preliminary hearing? They're going to force her to say her father did it. That's the end of her relationship with her father. And that's the end of your marriage. In case no one's told you, if Tom pleads guilty or a jury finds him guilty, he's going away to prison for a long time. And what are you going to do then, if that happens? And if you won't do it for them, then do it for yourself! Look at you! When was the last time you curled your hair? Or changed that dress? It's been at least a day. I saw you in it yesterday. This is all crumbing around you. Someone's got to stop it. And if you can't, I'm going to."

Linda's voice had been gradually growing more shrill. At last she stopped, her sister's shoulders slumped forward, her hands covering her face.

"Look, Marilyn, I don't want to make this all more miserable for you, more horrible than it already is. But we have to do something to stop this from happening. We at least have to try. We have to do it fast. Before the preliminary hearing. If this goes beyond the preliminary hearing, it might be too late. Do you understand?"

Marilyn Russell pulled her hands down to her chin.

"What can I do?"

"You don't have to do anything except come with me to talk to Travis Fuller. I want to level with him. Tell him what I'm thinking. Will you do that with me? Tomorrow, if he can see us?"

"You call him. I don't think I've got the energy to do it."

"I'm calling him first thing in the morning. Can you meet with him around noon?"

"I can take the afternoon off."

"Then I'll call you right after I talk to him."

"Have you seen Tom in the last couple of days?"

Marilyn shook her head.

"Maybe we can go visit tomorrow, after we talk to Fuller."

Linda walked to the sink and filled the teapot with fresh water. She hadn't told her sister she'd visited with Tom earlier that day. It was his look of despair, his complete emotional collapse, that had prompted the conversation this evening. Because the truth of the matter was that Linda feared the man was growing more suicidal as the days passed. It was imperative something, or someone, save him right now.

9

HER MOTHER AND the new weekend nurse's aide were huddled at the sink. The aide had a hairbrush in her hand and was holding a mirror up for Judith's mother to look at herself. "She's a new woman, Mrs. Thornton. A new woman!" The aide whirled her mother around to face Judith and for the first time she noticed her hair had been dyed blue.

Judith was startled awake. It was another bad dream. Not exactly a bad dream. Another bizarre dream about her mother. She seldom said anything in the dreams, just stared, or someone else did the talking. Judith never tried to make any sense of them individually, but as a whole they seemed to be about the same. Little things her mother did or said. Short vignettes. It was more Judith's funny little memories working their way into her sleep. She'd never touched her mother in the dreams. Never hugged her or got a hug from her. Someone told Judith once it was a symbol of bad luck if that happened.

She lay still a few moments, then turned to

the radio alarm. It was 6 o'clock. A busy day today, she thought, as she threw the covers to the side and sat at the edge of the bed. Tonight she and Elizabeth were going over to Annette's. It wasn't something Judith was looking forward to. It was unlike her to feel this way about a woman who up to now had been a good friend. She felt a twinge of guilt that eventually subsided. There was something of importance, aside from friendship, involved, and somehow this made it easier for her.

Marilyn and Linda sat in the small office that passed for Travis Fuller's conference room. Law books, mostly of California statutes, lined the walls. They waited only a few minutes before Fuller appeared, carrying a cup of coffee.

"Can I offer you ladies something to drink? A cup of coffee?"

They declined, feeling the pressure to get on with their concerns. It was Linda who carried the conversation.

"Mr. Fuller, we're here because I pressured Marilyn into coming. I'm frankly concerned the case is headed in a direction that can only end with Tom's conviction of something. But any way it ends, it's going to be disaster for Marilyn and the kids . . . and Tom. I want . . . I need to know if there's anything else we can do to help them. I'm concerned, I don't know just how to say this . . . I'm concerned this isn't your area of expertise."

The women weren't sure what to expect.

Perhaps he'd be insulted. Angry at having his abilities questioned.

"I understand what you're saying. In fact, I've already told Tom I didn't know if I could . . . or should . . . handle his case after the preliminary hearing is over. I suspect, all things being equal, and knowing the course of these serious felonies, that he is going to be bound over to Superior Court. I've laid it on the line with him, and I will with you. The DA's playing hardball with him. He pleads guilty before the preliminary hearing or he doesn't plead at all. It's standard operating procedure in the child molest cases. If the child takes the stand at the preliminary hearing and is put through the trauma of testifying, there's no deal afterward. In short, Tom's got to plead guilty."

"No! He can't do that! He didn't do it!"

Marilyn's reaction was swift and loud enough to bring Fuller's secretary to the door to ask if everything was okay.

"I understand your feelings, Mrs. Russell. You've got to understand my take on this. This isn't a complicated case. Not by a longshot. But if you're looking for someone else, maybe that you think can change the course of events. . . ."

"Nnn. . . ."

"We are, I think, Mr. Fuller." Linda's voice was strong, interrupting her sister before the conversation took them back to where they were when they entered the office. "We don't want you to feel we don't trust you. We need to be sure there's nothing else that we can do before it's too late."

Fuller shifted in his chair. "I'm glad if we're going to make any kind of change we're doing it now. I'm retained . . . paid by you, Mrs. Russell, so it might be easier to make the change you want. Let's do this. I don't want to tell the court or prosecutor about this just yet. We have a few days. We need to see if there's anyone who can take your case. It's not going to be easy to get someone to do that before the preliminary hearing."

"Do you have any names, people we can call?"

"A few. There are some formalities we have to go through with the court. If someone agrees to take the case, you might be able to get a continuance of the preliminary hearing. The court and prosecutor won't look too happily at that, since there's a child involved and they want her memory as intact as they can get it . . . you know how time can warp memory."

"I know how children's memories can be made to *become* warped over time," Marilyn blurted out.

"I have a name you might start with. Alan Larson. He's about the best. If anyone can come up with some way to help you, or at least get things slowed down a bit, he can do it. He's also very busy. I think he's just starting a death penalty case, and if that's so, you might not get him. Those capital cases grind an office to a halt for everything. But he's damn good. I've got some other people I can call for you, but let's check with Larson first. He takes appointed cases where the court appoints the attorney. But he might take you on what they call 'pro bono,' for free, if you will. He does some of that. This might be the kind of case he'd take like that. I'll call and ask him if he'd take a look at Tom's case."

By the time Marilyn and Linda stopped at the grocery store and arrived home, Marilyn had a message from Fuller on the answering machine. Fuller had talked with Larson. Larson, it seemed, had indeed started a death penalty case, and while he'd be happy to take a look at the file to see if there was anything else Fuller might want to try, he couldn't take the case himself.

10

THE LARGE BROWN envelope lay on Judith's chair, placed there by someone who didn't want his name advertised on the front, where neat black ink printed only, "To: Mrs. Thornton." Judith lifted it and realized from the weight and the way it shifted that it was a transcript of some kind. She opened the metal clasps at the top of the envelope and slipped the bound document halfway out. The small yellow tab stuck to the clear plastic cover and read simply, "This is the transcript you wanted to look at." Four other yellow tabs protruded from the sides of the four-hundred-page transcript, marking places in the text that someone thought were important.

Judith slipped the transcript back into the envelope and rose to close her office door. Returning to her desk, she quickly cleared it of mail and files that needed processing. Her desk top cleared, she removed the transcript from the envelope and slipped her finger in at the first yellow tab and began to read.

The transcript was the word-for-word ac-

count of the proceedings at trial. This trial
hadn't been one of the more notorious, but it
was certainly one of the most brutal the office
had prosecuted in some time. Two men kidnapping and raping college coeds, beating
them, and then dumping them on freeway ex-
its. They'd caught them before anyone had
been killed, but the trauma to the victims had
been considerable, and worse, they had had to
testify to each sordid detail of their ordeals.
The transcript pages marked were those where
the victims testified.

After years of prosecuting every kind of ver-
min, every kind of deranged hoodlum and
psychopath, Judith, although still outraged,
had developed the necessary objectivity in approach and treatment of brutality for presentation to a jury. Certainly, a secretary wouldn't
be able to handle the facts of these cases with
quite the same dispassionate analysis.

Judith recognized the handwriting on the
note. It was known immediately. It was the
transcript Mercer had the secretaries, Andrea
Bracken and Susan Middleton, read back to
him in private.

"My God," she murmured under her
breath, as she finished the last of the marked
passages. "How incredibly despicable."

For a moment or two it occurred to her that
the women might be mistaken. The man was
so honorable on the outside. So suave and
proper. Then she remembered: the grocery
store. The incident in the office. The leering.
The almost total lack of propriety.

Judith left the passages marked and slipped

the transcript back into the envelope. Then she put the entire transcript in the bottom drawer of her desk. Just what she'd do with it now was another matter. The secretaries involved would never complain about what Mercer was subjecting them to. If they were going to, they'd have done it by now. In any event, it would be hard to prove the man's motive was prurient. And if push came to shove, it might be a real power struggle. As for Judith, she wasn't going to push the matter. Not now, anyway. The transcript and her knowledge of its misuse were sensitive matters. If someone brought a complaint and the charges were proved, *no, even if the charges were just made,* it could ruin the man.

"Hey, Jude!" The knock on her office door and sudden appearance of Mercer startled Judith. She felt her face redden. "Turkey Shoot time. You coming?"

Judith looked at her desk clock. She was late for the meeting known affectionately in the office as the "Turkey Shoot." Despite its awkwardly humorous name, the meeting was intended to allow the prosecuting attorneys a chance to look at the newly filed cases and weed out those that had low probability of successful prosecution due to loss of evidence, folding witnesses, or simple lack of evidence. The cases, the "turkeys," were analyzed and decisions were made about whether they should be prosecuted.

Judith quickly followed Mercer down the hallway to the conference room where seven or eight files awaited the reviewing deputies.

One by one they were discussed, the prosecuting attorney or police investigator taking the lead in summarizing the case for the others.

"Okay, let's see. The next one is the Thomas Russell case. Aaron, I think that's yours." Judith's eyes were suddenly riveted on Mercer. She hadn't expected to see the case here in conference. Were the case weaknesses now as noticeable to others as they were to her?

Mercer removed the elastic band from the file folder and took a videotape from it.

"Some of you are already aware of this case. It's a child molest-rape. The defendant is the victim's father. Judith has been adamant and quite vocal in her beliefs that the case shouldn't go to trial. Isn't that right, Jude?" He didn't wait for her to respond. Everyone in the room knew Mercer and Judith were at loggerheads over the case. "After consulting with Larry, it was our decision to go forward with the prosecution, even though the child says it isn't her father who molested her. The case is serious enough and the implications of not prosecuting are so potentially harmful to the office that we felt the case has to proceed at least to the preliminary hearing stage. It's not a weak case by any stretch of the imagination. But there is more evidence that ought to be analyzed carefully, and I thought perhaps you all might be able to help."

Mercer walked to the video set in the corner of the room and switched on the television.

"This is a tape of the last session the victim, Caryn Russell, had with her child psychologist. It was filmed at the psychologist's office."

The room fell silent as Mercer turned the sound up. Only Caryn Russell and a middle-aged woman with black hair piled high at the forehead and whipped into a bun at the back of her head were present. Caryn sat on the floor playing with a large dollhouse and several small dolls. Most of the attorneys knew the dolls were being used to represent Caryn and her family members.

"Now, Caryn," the woman said in a soothing voice, "where are you in the house?"

The little girl pushed the dollhouse away from the wall closer to herself.

"I'm here in the bedroom."

"Where's the rest of your family?"

"They're in the other bedrooms."

"Can you put them in the rooms they were in when you were hurt?"

The girl carefully pushed a male doll and a female doll into one bedroom. Another male doll was pushed into a second bedroom. The girl doll was placed in yet a third bedroom.

"I need another doll," Caryn said, looking up at the woman.

"What kind of doll do you need, Caryn?"

"A man doll."

"Is that a doll that is anyone you know?"

"No. He's the man who was in my room."

The psychologist gave no information and was careful not to judge what the girl was telling her. She changed the subject slightly.

"Caryn, if you had to make your house more safe, how would you do that?"

Without pausing, the girl pulled the house

even closer to herself and checked the window to the bedroom where the doll representing her had been placed. Then she scooted the house across the floor to the wall and pushed her window up against it, clearly creating a barrier to entry into her room.

"How is that going to keep you safer, Caryn?" the psychologist asked.

"Now, no one can come into my bedroom. And the man can't kill anyone."

"What man, Caryn?"

"The man who hurt me. The one who came into my bedroom through the window and said he'd kill everyone in my house if I told anyone."

"Thank you, Caryn. Why don't we leave the dolls here and go get some lunch?"

The tape ended abruptly. After a moment the unsolicited comments from around the room started.

"I'd say the little girl there doesn't think it was anyone in her family that hurt her."

"I agree."

Judith didn't comment. Her feelings about the case seemed to be vindicated.

"Well, I'd have agreed—except that tape was made a few weeks ago," Mercer added. "Here's the one made two days ago."

It took a moment to slip the second tape into the video machine. It was the same setting, the same psychologist with Caryn. This time, however, there was no play therapy. The girl was seated at a table across from a man Judith recognized immediately as a police investigator.

"Caryn, can you tell me where your father was the night you were hurt?"

There was no answer at first, then the girl spoke, almost under her breath.

"I'm not sure."

"Could he have been in your bedroom?"

"I . . . I'm not sure. Anymore."

Mercer snapped the video off. Judith couldn't contain herself.

"What happened to that little girl between the tapes, Aaron? How come she's so sure her father didn't do it, in fact needed to be protected, in one tape, and then in the next doesn't know where he was when she was hurt?"

"You see, Judith, that's my problem. That's why I wanted the rest of the office to look at the case with us today. At least look at these tapes with us. It seems to me the first tape hurts the prosecution, but you know how difficult children can be. She doesn't want to identify her father as the man who assaulted her. I've decided she's protecting him, and I don't mean from some burglar. I realize you feel differently."

"What's the psychologist say?" Judith asked.

"She says the girl's suffering from some kind of stress disorder. They don't believe her story about some stranger coming into the house, then leaving again."

"I, for one, would have to say you go forward with the case, Aaron."

"I think my feelings are the same," added another voice.

Judith sighed audibly. "Is there any other evidence that would tend to exonerate the father?" she asked.

There was only the briefest of pauses. "Not that I'm aware of, Jude. You know I'd turn that over to the defense." For the moment, at least, the existence of Arthur Whaley and his similar assaults near the Russell home were submerged deep in the recesses of Aaron Mercer's memory.

One of the deputies sitting next to Judith spoke next. "If you're asking if you should go with the prosecution, I'd say yes. Take it through the preliminary hearing, and if he won't plead, all bets are off after the hearing and bindover."

"That's exactly what I've offered," Mercer said pointedly.

"What if he's not guilty?" Judith added. "What if Caryn's first version of the story is the correct one?"

Mercer walked over to Judith and stood directly in front of her. "We've had this discussion before, Judith." There was the condescension again. The father-scolding-child tone.

Judith didn't respond. She didn't stand or contradict his comments, but simply watched as he walked back over to the television, removed the videos, and left the room. There was no need to bring the case here to the conference. Mercer'd already decided he was going to prosecute. This was no plea for prosecutorial advice from colleagues. No. He'd staged this to put her in her place.

"What's the next case about?" someone asked.

Before Judith could think to respond or leave the room, there was a voice behind her.

"Mrs. Thornton?"

It was her secretary.

"There's an emergency of some kind down in Department Fourteen, Superior Court."

Department 14 was the courtroom where the serial murderer George Mons was being tried. It was a death penalty case, being handled by one of the office's most experienced prosecutors, Tyler Olson.

"Who's calling in the emergency?" Judith asked.

"Olson is. In fact, he's up in his office now. He says he needs to see you right away. It can't wait."

"Tell him I'll be right there. No, better yet, I'll go see him right now."

When she reached Olson's office, Judith found several deputies gathered around his desk. When she arrived, the deputies excused themselves and left.

"What's the problem, Tyler?"

"I sort of got kicked out of the trial, that's what's the problem."

"How can you sort of get kicked out of a trial?"

"It wasn't really me who did anything. Larson had some kind of urgent problem he needed to talk to the judge about, without my being present. He asked to approach the judge, and old man Bright called him up to the sidebar for a minute, then the judge and

Larson went into chambers with the court reporter. Fifteen minutes later they come back into court and send me out. The judge closes the courtroom to everyone, even the press, and sends the jury home until tomorrow afternoon."

"What about the second defense counsel?"

In every death penalty case the defendant was entitled by statute to two attorneys. The Mons case was no different.

"Second counsel stayed on in the courtroom, too."

Judith was calm. Although her colleague was excited and somewhat flustered, she was skeptical. Alan Larson was no stranger to Judith. He'd been her nemesis in more than one trial. A brilliant defense attorney, he stopped at nothing to exonerate his clients, at times skirting what she considered to be the bounds of propriety and legal ethics. As far as she knew, this could just be one of his antics designed to delay the trial or force reversible error into the record.

"Are you sure this isn't one of Larson's tactics?"

"How am I supposed to tell if it is? The court took him pretty seriously."

"Judges take everything seriously in a death penalty trial."

"The problem with Larson is he's brilliant. And he's willing to skirt the edges. I've seen the man pull some pretty incredible stunts to get a client off. But if the judge is taking this much time, there's a problem. Who's the second defense attorney?" The question was important. Some were far better than others. If Larson's position in the case was somehow compromised, the second was going to have to be strong enough to carry the case."

"Is the judge going to call back when some kind of conclusion is reached about whatever it is that's bothering everyone?"

"He said he'd call me back into court."

"I want you to let me know when that happens, Tyler. Don't get too excited. It's undoubtedly one of Larson's tricks. I want to be there when this gets back under way. I wouldn't trust Alan Larson as far as I could see him. Then I'd still be wondering if what I saw was correct."

"God, Judith, he's excellent. I haven't heard cross-examination like his in a while."

"He's a great attorney all right, if you define great attorneys by their win ratio. He doesn't like losing in court. I've seen him pose as a prosecution investigator and punch holes in the courtroom paper cups to embarrass the opposing witnesses and attorneys. So I'm not making any judgments about how serious this matter is until I find out what it's about. Call me as soon as you know what's happening down there."

The call came an hour later. Judith's presence was requested in Department 14. When she arrived, aside from the court reporter, bailiff, and clerk, only her deputy, Tyler Olson, the defendant, George Mons, and Alan Larson were present. The bailiff was standing behind

the defendant, who was handcuffed and at-
tired in a yellow jail jumpsuit. With the jury
excused, his jail attire was acceptable. The trial
judge hadn't taken the bench.

Judith took a seat at the prosecutor's counsel
table with Olson.

"Where's the judge?" she asked.

"He's in chambers, taking a look at the cases
Larson's given him."

"And second defense counsel?"

"He's been excused for now so as not to be
tainted by whatever it is that's at issue. Have
you ever seen anything like this before, Judith?"

"Well, I'm not quite sure what I'm seeing
yet. I do know one thing, I'm not letting Larson off the hook in this one. The order of business here is holding his feet to the fire. As far
as I'm concerned, at this point it's another of
his delaying tactics."

As she ended her comment, she glanced
over toward the defense counsel table where
Larson and Mons were engaged in a heated
discussion. She'd never totally disliked Larson. In fact, she respected his trial abilities.
She'd never do the kinds of things he did to
win cases though. But then, she'd never been
a defense attorney. She didn't know what she
might do if she were and a client who she believed in actually was not guilty. What lengths
might she go to to save him.

Larson rose from the counsel table and
walked to where she was seated.

"Judith. I'm sorry you have to be dragged
down here. We have a hell of a problem. At

least, *I* have a hell of a problem. I'm afraid you're not going to get many of the specifics today because of the nature of the problem. You're going to have to trust me on this one." There was the briefest of pauses before he smiled. "At least, you're going to have to trust the judge on this one."

Judith smiled back. "I'd feel more comfortable trusting the judge, Alan."

With this, the door at the back of the judge's bench opened and Judge William Winston entered. With only the defendant and counsel present in court, he'd abandoned use of his bailiff to announce his arrival. Winston was a newcomer to the Superior Court. Forty-five and athletic, he had a legal practice which had been confined to civil cases involving principally land use issues. Having been on the bench for two years, though, he'd made his largest impact in the criminal area and now was assigned exclusively to high-profile defendants. His was a firm, steady hand that seldom lost control to the attorneys, a significant value in death penalty cases where the first item of business was who, the court or defense counsel, was going to control the proceedings.

"First, I want to be sure the record reflects all counsel are present, as is the defendant, Mr. Mons. Mr. Larson is here, and the court has excused his co-counsel, at least for purposes of this hearing. We've been joined by Mrs. Thornton from the District Attorney's Office. I asked for your presence, Mrs. Thornton, because we have a legal issue that's arisen here and any input we can have would be greatly appreciated, given the serious nature of this case. I'm going to keep this discussion at a general level to protect the defense. Some might believe neither you nor your attorney, Mr. Olson, should be here at all. But I think we can keep the discussion on a legal level here."

Judith rose to address the court.

"Your Honor, may I make a brief statement?"

"Certainly, Mrs. Thornton."

"My initial concern is whether this matter will be delaying the trial needlessly."

"I can assure you, Mrs. Thornton," the judge interjected, "this is not a delaying tactic by Mr. Larson. If I had even the briefest concern that that was the case, you wouldn't be here."

"Thank you, Your Honor, but I've been party to more death penalty delays than I care to summarize for the court. . . ."

"Then don't. Mrs. Thornton, you're going to have to trust me on this one."

Judith looked quickly toward Larson. He wasn't smiling. She'd have to trust the judge.

"Okay, Your Honor, I can do that."

As she took her seat again, the judge opened several casebooks to pages someone had previously marked for him.

"Let's see. I think I'll summarize this for the benefit of Mrs. Thornton and Mr. Olson. Mr. Larson, correct me if I misspeak. Now, as I understand it, a conflict has risen between Mr. Larson and Mr. Mons. This is not a tactical conflict. It doesn't involve a choice of what defense is best or what witnesses are going to be put on in what order, that kind of thing. It involves an ethical conflict. It appears Mr. Mons wants to testify and Mr. Larson does not want him to testify. Is that right so far, Mr. Larson?"

"Yes, Your Honor, it is. As you know, because I've already put it on the record, I can't disclose the nature issue itself because that's privileged between Mr. Mons and me. But I'm in a spot. I can't and won't call Mr. Mons to testify even though he wants very much to testify on his own behalf."

The judge turned to Mons. "Is that correct, Mr. Mons?"

"Yes, Your Honor, it is. I. . . ."

"Stop right there, Mr. Mons!" the judge interjected, holding his hand up to emphasize the point. "Don't say anything more than I ask you."

"Your Honor," Larson added, "if the matter were tactical, I'd defer to my client's wishes and let him testify. This isn't tactical. It is a matter where I believe I am ethically barred from calling him."

Judith wanted to respond, but to what? The ethical matter was Larson's call. There weren't many issues that could cause something this significant. One was that Larson knew his client wasn't going to tell the truth. The rules of ethical conduct prohibited suborning perjury. Yet as far as she knew, the right to testify in one's own defense was still an essential part of the due process rights guaranteed in the federal Constitution.

"Good God," she whispered to Olson. "Larson has a true ethics issue here. I never thought I'd see that."

"What do you think it is?" Olson responded in a hushed voice.

"I suspect it has something to do with whether his client's going to tell the truth."

The judge, who'd been reading the cases set out for him on his bench, looked up and turned to Judith.

"Mrs. Thornton, I realize this is hard, given that you haven't the foggiest idea what's at issue here, but I just need to ask you whether you are aware of any cases dealing with whether an attorney who has an ethical conflict calling a defendant to the stand must accede to his client's wishes to testify. Who wins in that case?"

"I'm not sure, Your Honor. The defendant could simply give a narrative. That is, just take the stand and talk."

"I could never allow that, Your Honor," Larson added. "In short, there's no easy way out of this for me. I must ask the court to release me from this case and allow the defendant to testify on his own behalf. If I am allowed to continue his representation or he is kept from taking the stand, I think we have reversible error and this case is going to have to be retried."

There was a loud sigh from the judge. "As much as I hate to admit it, I think Mr. Larson has a point."

"But Your Honor, I think this places the trial of Mr. Mons in a terrible posture. If Mr. Larson's been his chief attorney, as I know he has, then what do we tell the jury? What about the continuity of the trial for the prosecution? I suspect if we now release Mr. Larson from this trial and it goes on, Mr. Mons is going to object that his own trial has been irreparably damaged." She looked over toward Larson. The courtroom was silent for a moment, and Larson rose.

"Your Honor, there is no easy way out for me. I must be removed from the case. But if that happens, my client will certainly be jeopardized before this jury. We will have to ask for a mistrial. We, unfortunately, will have to start all over. With a new jury being selected. We do that now, or in three years, after the case is reversed on appeal. That has to be my position, Judge."

Judith was now beyond irritation; she was angry. She'd been conferring with Olson every step of the way. The case had been proceeding without a hitch. They liked the jury. The three victim-witnesses who'd survived Mons's attacks had testified and identified him in court. If they had to start over again, all of that would be gone.

"Mrs. Thornton, what have you and Mr. Olson to say?"

Judith leaned toward her deputy.

"You take it, Judith. I think whatever has to be said should come from the office."

Judith rose to address the court.

"My concern is delay, Your Honor. These death penalty cases take years to try, then years to appeal. I need to be certain the interests of society in general. . . ."

"You can save the speeches about public policy, Mrs. Thornton. I know them. This isn't a public policy issue here. This is an inescapable conflict. One I don't want to see taint this trial all the way through. I'll take the heat in the press. I need a brief recess to think this through one last time. Don't go away, anyone."

When the judge left, Larson remained strangely quiet. He whispered to Mons and wrote on the white-lined pad of paper on the desk before him. Fifteen minutes later the judge took the bench, and after noting the presence of all parties to the action, began his ruling.

"I've struggled with the issue before us and have come to the conclusion there is an irreconcilable conflict presented between the defendant's Sixth Amendment right to testify on his own behalf and his attorney's ethical decision not to call him to the stand. There are compromises available, but none that Mr. Larson is comfortable with. Now, I realize there is no guarantee that this isn't going to happen again with another counsel. Mrs. Thornton and Mr. Olson are probably thinking, 'What's to keep this Mr. Mons from pulling this stunt again if another jury is impaneled?' The answer to that is, nothing can keep it from happening again. But if it does, there's a track record we can look to. If it happened again, perhaps some kind of compromise would have to be worked out. I think Mr. Larson and Mr. Mons understand, and I would not look favorably on this issue arising again without some kind of remedial action being taken by me. I certainly have no intention of allowing Mr. Mons to start and end trial whenever he wanted. You understand that, Mr. Mons?"

The defendant was grinning and nodding. He'd won and he knew it. In stark contrast, Larson sat silent and unsmiling at his side.

"Answer out loud, Mr. Mons."

"I understand, Judge."

Judith was listening, but she realized too that if this was a true ethical conflict involving the defendant's telling the truth, all he'd have to do is tell his next attorney what he'd told Larson, and the same issue would arise. And she wasn't so sure any compromise could be struck with the Sixth Amendment of the Constitution.

"Do you have anything to say, Mr. Larson?"

"No, Judge, I'm assuming you are declaring a mistrial?"

"I am. Mrs. Thornton, Mr. Olson? Anything to add?"

"Just that I'd prefer to see Mr. Larson remain on this case with a narrative testimony by the defendant."

"Okay, I will declare a mistrial. We'll need the jury brought back as soon as we can get them, Madame Clerk. Mrs. Thornton, thank you for coming down on such short notice. We are adjourned until the jury is reassembled. When they're here, we'll call you."

With this, the judge gathered the books on

his bench and left the courtroom. Mons was quickly removed by the bailiff.

"Judith," Larson called, as she was about to leave through the doors to the hallway. "I'm truly sorry about this. I didn't want to give up this case."

He sounded almost sincere. But she couldn't help feeling that beneath the righteousness, he was certainly pleased the case was delayed. For whatever reasons, the delay had occurred. And so her response was pleasant but sarcastic.

"I'd have preferred you remained on the case, Alan. I guess this means you're unemployed."

11

AT 7 O'CLOCK Judith and Elizabeth rang the doorbell at Annette's house. Annette's daughter intercepted them and the two girls disappeared down the hallway. Annette's mother showed Judith into the living room.

"I'm so sorry Annette's not up and about. It's so inconvenient for her to be in the living areas of the house. I'll go down and see if she's ready to visit. It might take a few minutes."

"That's okay! Tell her not to hurry. I don't have any time I need to be anywhere."

Judith found a comfortable chair and settled in, looking around the room at the baby pictures and family portraits. Annette was an artist in the truest sense of the word. Not only could she paint and sketch, everything she touched was art, was made more beautiful. Some people just had that ability. Whether it was tying a simple bow on a present or setting crackers around the plate, it was all done with a flair that seemed so natural to Annette, yet most people had to work at it. The bow looked two sizes bigger. The crackers somehow were all uniformly placed, pointing in the same direction. And nothing was done simply if it involved her daughter. Birthday parties had that extra measure of effort. One year Annette had actually handpainted a watercolor pillow for each child. The pillows each had an animal beginning with the first name of the child guest. Elizabeth received an elephant which was so beautiful that Judith put it up in her own closet for a year, until Elizabeth could appreciate the artistry.

Fifteen minutes passed before Annette came into the room. It seemed to Judith that she shuffled, her bedroom slippers scraping along the hardwood floor of the hallway to the living room. Behind her she pulled her metal respirator, the way one might pull a piece of wheeled luggage. On her head she wore a scarf wrapped as a turban. Judith got out of the chair and gave her a hug.

"Pardon my hat in the house," Annette said, smiling slightly. "It's keeping my head warm. It's because of the chemotherapy. I was hoping I'd have some hair back again before now."

"Does that go everywhere with you?" Judith asked, motioning toward the respirator.

"Everywhere, now. I need it to breathe, and it's got my medication attached. There's no limit on how much of it I take now. Just whenever I want. However much I want."

The two women sat, Annette taking the large chair Judith had been sitting in while she waited.

"Can you pull that ottoman over, Judith?" she asked.

Judith complied, realizing the woman was in pain only when she tried to lift her legs onto it and could not do so without assistance from Judith.

At last comfortable, the women talked at first about the things they always talked about when they met. How the children were doing, what Annette's husband, a commercial pilot, was up to in his job, what was happening in the soccer club. On reflection later, it seemed to Judith that it took a while for the subject matter to shift to Annette's long-term condition. It wasn't good. The cancer had spread beyond what any of the doctors could control. It was in her lymph system and several vital organs, including her liver. With any luck, she had several months, but it was probably much less than that.

Annette's tone was flat, neither desperate nor emotional. And this, too, surprised Judith. She hadn't known how she would react to seeing Annette so ill. But the woman kept the visit on an objective level.

"Mark's in New York. He'll be home tomorrow. That's part of the reason I wanted you to come today, Judith. It's just easier to talk when he's not here. I can handle everything until he's here, then, I don't know, it's more difficult. The dynamics with everything change. And he and my sister seem to be getting in each other's way. I'm stuck in the middle. I need them both so desperately. But there are some things I need to have done. Mark has his ideas about everything. And so does my family. I want to be sure things are . . . the way

I want them at the end, Judith. I'm not sure who I can ask. I don't want to go to a lawyer."

"You need my help with some legal matters?"

"I want you to be Sarah's legal guardian. If anything happens to Mark."

Judith was silent just long enough for Annette to understand the depth of her surprise. The two women had been close friends, but not with the closeness one might expect from someone you wanted to permanently entrust your child to.

"I, I don't know what to say, Annette."

"I know this is probably a surprise to you, Judith. But I'm serious about it. I don't think you'll ever have to worry about it taking effect. Mark's got a good safety record." The last comment drew a laugh from her, and she caught herself grimacing with pain, originating at which part of her body she didn't give away. She reached for the canister of oxygen and pushed a button. In a moment or two she relaxed and was able to resume talking.

"I love my family dearly. But I don't want them raising Sarah. There are lots of reasons. But the bottom line is, I don't think they can do it very well. I want her going to college. Knowing how to handle money. You can't see it now, but their lifestyles have a lot to be desired. Too much liquor. Too much travel. Do this for me, Judith?"

"Well, sure, I'll do it. I don't want anyone mad at me."

"They won't be mad at you. They might be confused for a while. They're having a very tough time with this all. It's only going to get worse. But I don't think I could be happy unless this gets taken care of. It's such an important thing to me right now."

"Are you really sure, Annette? My lifestyle's not all that terrific."

Her friend laughed. "Your only problem, Judith, is, you're too cerebral. It's not like I haven't tried. I've been dropping hints to Gareth that you're available."

"Gareth?"

"Pretending you don't notice him? The soccer coach?"

Judith blushed.

"Your face is turning red, Judith. You need to talk to the man. He's not married, you know. I asked. On your behalf, of course. So I've done what I can. The rest is up to you. I suppose you'll have to be thinking about Sarah's future now if she were motherless and fatherless." She laughed and gave herself another dose of medication.

"Stop talking like that, Annette. You're still here, and you're going to be here a long time."

"No, I won't be. I can feel myself getting weaker." She pointed to the canister. "And it's taking more of this stuff here to make me comfortable. Oh! I almost forgot."

Annette shoved her hand into the pocket of her robe and retrieved a small black velvet box.

"I want you to have this, Judith. It's a remembrance of me, and it would mean a lot to me for you to have it. And don't argue with me about it, please. Do this for me."

Judith took the box from her and opened it. Inside was a diamond tennis bracelet.

"I can't take this, Annette!"

"Don't you remember when I got this, Judith?"

"Sure, I do. We were shopping and it was on sale. After Christmas, two years ago. It was, if I remember, going to be your present to yourself."

"Well, I've left all my jewelry for Sarah. It's in a safe deposit box. This one thing, though, has a meaning all its own. I want you to have it. It would make me happy if you took it. To remember me, you know. You can't turn down a dying woman's last request now, can you?"

Annette laughed as Judith's eyes filled with tears and then overflowed onto her cheeks. Judith clumsily wiped them from her cheeks with her hands, then fumbled for a tissue in her purse.

When she'd recovered herself, the conversation returned to Annette's request.

"When can I talk with your sister and Mark about your plans for Sarah? I should have some kind of conversation with them about it, if for no other reason than to let them know your wishes on it."

"Good luck. Mark wants his brother as Sarah's legal guardian. Of course, my sister wants that honor. She's going to be greatly offended when she discovers what I've done. I want you to get me the papers right away, Judith. I'm not feeling well, I told you that. It's

a major effort even to get out of bed anymore."

"I'll do what I can as fast as I can, Annette.
In fact, I'll give you a call tomorrow. I think I
can get to my probate attorney and have her
draw something up fast. I want you to look at
it. And Mark, I . . ."

"No, I want you to get it drawn up, Judith,
and bring it to me. I need to persuade Mark
somehow to sign it. This is a very sore spot
we have here that I have to get taken care of.
Can you help me?"

"I will, Annette. I promise."

Suddenly, Annette relaxed in the chair,
looking tired and gaunt. Judith glanced at her
wristwatch.

"It's nine-thirty. I've got to get home and
you've got to get some rest."

"Before you go, Judith, can I see Elizabeth?
I wanted to see her."

She knew what Annette wanted. She
wanted to say good-bye to Elizabeth. Judith
rose, a feeling of finality in her movements.
She recognized the feeling well. It was when
you know every move you make with another
person is the last. Not like the finality of di-
vorce or farewells after vacations about to end.
Recognizing the finality of death when it's
upon you, moving toward you—

"Don't get cerebral on me again, Judith. I
just want to see her to say goodnight."

Judith smiled and nodded.

"I'll get her, Annette."

*   *   *

Alan Larson was wrapping up his death penalty case. His office was in a shambles even after three hours of summarizing evidence and cataloging his own findings and documents. It was 10 P.M. and he still had hours of this to do. He was determined to complete the task tonight, even if he had to sleep at his office. There was no wife, there were no children to interfere with his tasks.

Another pot of coffee was what he needed. He stood, stretched, and paced around his desk. He was glad to be off the case. Although one side of him felt the victory of having had a death penalty case start over again, there was another side of Larson that was glad the judge had removed him. Mons was guilty. He'd told Larson that early on in the case. What he hadn't told Larson until a day earlier was that he wanted to testify and he was going to commit perjury when he was called to the stand. Larson had immediately rebelled against the idea. He couldn't in good conscience put the man on the stand, having been told beforehand that he was going to lie. That was suborning perjury, and if it became known that he was aware of it, his license was at stake. Still, he believed his client had the right to make the call about testifying on his own behalf. It was a constitutional right, and Larson would go down fighting for that. It was okay that once in a very great while he got to make a purely ethical call and feel good about it. Despite the uproar and chaos this was causing him, he felt good about the outcome.

Mons was now someone else's problem. God help them!

Box after box of documents and trial materials were piled against the wall next to Larson's door. Whoever took over the case would want and need an update in the forensics evidence and Larson was determined to finish it. But he needed a break. Another cup of coffee, maybe. As he reached for his coffeepot, he noticed a file he'd put at the corner of the credenza. He picked it up and walked back to his desk. It was the Thomas Russell case he'd promised Travis Fuller he'd look at. Perhaps a few minutes. It would be a good break—

It took only that long for Larson to realize what Fuller had suspected, or he wouldn't have asked him to look at the file. Fuller was in over his head. Larson pulled a pad of paper from his desk drawer and began to take notes. Where were the forensics? Hadn't anyone ordered a DNA test? What about the girl's story? Where were the shrinks' reports on the girl? On Russell? Caryn Russell's story was interesting, but far from unique. Of course, Travis Fuller wouldn't know that if he had only drunk driving cases to compare it to. Most notable was the lack of medical evidence connecting the father as perpetrator. The list of "where is its" went on for two pages. Not only was the case weak, the prosecutor was Aaron Mercer. Larson shook his head. Fuller versus Mercer. The thought was almost humorous. Mercer would chew him up and spit him out before he'd realized any bite had been taken.

Larson had seen Mercer at work. He re-

spected the man's abilities in court. He was
tough. Skilled. Smooth. He liked winning, too.
But there was a difference between him and
Mercer. He, Larson, was charged with making
the system do its job. Granted, he made it hard
for the system. Maybe put it through hoops,
even. But still, that was what defense attorneys
were supposed to do. He pushed the envelope.
But maybe one in a thousand clients needed
that pushing. Maybe one in a thousand clients
was actually innocent. God, half the time they
didn't even know if they were innocent. That
was Larson's real job. Keeping the one in a
thousand innocent people out of prison.

Mercer was the opposite of him. Mercer
made sure everyone, *everyone*, was found
guilty. He was a machine. A conviction machine. Win at all costs. But therein lay Mercer's
vice, and it was reprehensible to Larson. Mercer was a prosecutor, and prosecutors were
never supposed to convict the innocent. They
were supposed to avoid it at all costs. The
whole system was set up to allow the guilty
man to go free rather than convict an innocent
man. As good an attorney as Mercer was, he
never had accepted this responsibility, this re-
ality of the system. Mercer's whole existence
thrived on conviction of all. He was the equiv-
alent of Larson in the prosecutor's chair. He
let the Fullers of the world stumble over their
own feet. The Russell case in front of him was
an excellent example. It was a mess that any
competent prosecutor could see was heading
for certain conviction on a record that

screamed out for more investigation before any conviction was allowed.

When he stopped writing and sat back in his chair, Larson's back ached and his head was beginning to hurt. It was 1 A.M. Unless someone intervened quickly, Thomas Russell was about to be washed away in the current of trial procedure. There'd be a preliminary hearing and then a plea, because even if Fuller believed his client was innocent, he wouldn't know how to put the trial on. Worse, Russell might plead before the preliminary hearing without any investigation. Mercer, Larson knew, must surely be enjoying this.

Larson closed the file and set it on top of his briefcase. He was no longer unemployed.

12

ALAN LARSON WASTED no time the following morning. The first order of business was to divest himself of the Mons case. This he accomplished easily enough by calling a service to deliver his boxes of documents and notes to the attorney who'd served as second counsel to him. This done, he called Travis Fuller to tell him he would be able to take on the Russell case. Fuller was neither happy nor saddened to hear of his availability. It was his wish, though, that the transfer of the case be done quickly—before the preliminary hearing, if possible. With this Larson concurred. However, given what he saw as major deficiencies in the record, Larson was adamant that he needed a continuance. Since Fuller had been retained, there was a better chance of allowing a change of attorney than if he'd been appointed by the court.

Fuller volunteered to draft the motion requesting a change of counsel. They could only hope Mercer would agree. Without his agreement, it would be a tougher battle, but Larson was sure that if push came to shove, he could get the court to agree to the delay.

"Can you cover for Mercer?"

The calendar deputy was calling from the presiding department of the Superior Court, where it seemed the judge was prepared to consider Travis Fuller's request for a delay in the Russell preliminary hearing.

Aaron Mercer would normally have been served with the request and probably was. Unfortunately, he'd been called away on a family matter of some urgency and wouldn't be back until the afternoon.

"Can't you cover for him?" Judith asked the anxious deputy.

"No way. I've got strict orders. No calendar deputy touches Aaron's cases. I asked the judge to delay this until Aaron can be present. But it's not a serious offender case. And Fuller's pushing on it."

"Can you tell me anything about the motion?"

"Just that Fuller wants out. And your favorite defense counsel, Alan Larson, wants in. That's why they need the delay. New attorney coming on board."

"Larson?"

"Seems he's got some time on his hands now and has agreed to take this case. Aaron's going to have his hands full. Larson's already started asking for the reports he says Aaron's got to have somewhere. I don't have the file, or I'd see what's in there. I need someone else to handle this one, Judith, and I don't have any other line deputy I can call. I called Farrell. He said to call you. I do know how Aaron would feel about this delay."

"Me too."

"Can you handle it?"

"Someone's got to. Is there any way to delay this until Aaron's back?"

"I tried. No way. Judge wants to hear the matter in about ten minutes."

"I'll be down."

The Presiding Department of Superior Court was the courtroom through which all cases flowed. They were assigned out from there to the individual judges, and if there was no trial department available the presiding judge, Cleveland Turnquist, heard the matters himself. Efficiency above all prevailed.

Judith arrived, out of breath, and clutching a legal pad and a pen. She'd tried to find the Russell file on Mercer's desk, to no avail. She had only the most general of arguments to make on the office's behalf.

As she moved to the desk, abandoned to her for the moment by the calendar deputy, she noticed Larson and Fuller seated with the defendant at the counsel table to her right. She was barely able to rest before the court addressed her case.

"Next, let's hear the People versus Thomas Russell. Counsel are present, as is Mr. Russell. Mrs. Thornton's here for Mr. Mercer."

"Well, Your Honor, preliminarily, I'm not here for Mr. Mercer. He doesn't know about this hearing, and I'm afraid he's not going to be happy it's being held without him."

The court ignored her concerns about Mercer's sensitivity.

"Mrs. Thornton, I have a request here from Mr. Fuller to be relieved as counsel on the case of *People versus Thomas Russell*. The preliminary hearing is set for five days from today. Mr. Fuller is asking for a delay. The court would wait for Mr. Mercer's return, as your deputy asked, but in looking at the court's file, I see no reason to put the matter over. What kind of problem's going to be caused because of a two-week delay?"

"We have a child witness in the case, Your Honor. As in all child-victim cases, we want to get the matter to trial or disposed of as quickly as we can."

"We all do, Mrs. Thornton. Is there really any reason not to give Mr. Russell two weeks?"

Judith turned toward Larson.

"Actually, Your Honor, no. There's not. The People will agree to a two-week delay to allow Mr. Larson to get caught up. I suspect Your Honor would have granted the request."

The judge smiled. "I might have. Then again, I always like brisk argument, Mrs. Thornton. Then again, it's refreshing to simply do what's right. You gentlemen agreeable to two weeks?"

"I think that's going to be sufficient, Judge," Fuller said. "I am going to formally request to be removed from the case. Mr. Larson will next appear for Mr. Russell."

"Mr. Russell, you do not have to consent to this delay. You have a right to have your preliminary hearing set as it is. Do you understand that?"

"Yes."

His voice was barely audible.

"Louder, Mr. Russell, I didn't hear you," the court repeated.

"Yes. I understand."

"And you agree to the two-week delay?"

"Yes, I agree to it."

"Then two weeks it is."

Larson then rose to address the court.

"Your Honor, I think there's discovery—medical reports, police reports—that we don't have."

"Have they been requested, Mr. Larson?"

Larson turned to Fuller, who was seated next to him. Fuller shook his head.

"Mr. Fuller's shaking his head 'no,' which indicates to me that they haven't been asked for, Mr. Larson. Ask for them. Then complain to me if you don't get them. Anything else, gentlemen and lady?"

No one spoke.

"Thank you, then. And my regards to Mr. Mercer, Mrs. Thornton."

A sigh of relief followed the judge's departure into his chambers. The three attorneys stood a moment staring at the empty bench. Fuller shook hands with Larson and promised to call him that evening. Larson turned to his new client and said a few words of encouragement, then, as Russell was led away by the bailiff, Larson turned to Judith.

"Thanks, Judith. It made it easier," Larson whispered, as he packed his briefcase.

"God help me, now I have Aaron to deal with," was her only response. "When he gets word I agreed to a continuance. . . ."

"You know I couldn't have taken this case if you'd been successful yesterday. I'd still be down the hall with Mr. Mons."

The irony of the situation hit her. "Well, the Lord does work in mysterious ways, now, doesn't He, Mr. Larson?"

His briefcase packed, Larson passed her desk and leaned toward her.

"He sure does, Mrs. Thornton. And from the looks of this file . . . have you seen it?"

Judith froze. It was beyond any obligation or concern of hers to comment on another deputy's case.

"If you've looked at our office file, you know I have, Alan."

"I asked for it this morning and took a look. You had the case originally, Judith. Word has it you wanted to dump it."

"No comment."

"Why'd you want to dump it, Judith?" he whispered, his face close enough to force her eyes to his.

"You know I can't comment."

"There's no case here. It's a Mercer special. Why won't he kick it?"

"Why won't Aaron kick anything? Look, I'm going to be in deep enough when he finds out I've given you, of all people, two weeks to catch up with him."

"Like I said, thanks."

As Larson turned to leave, Judith called out after him.

"Good luck, Alan."

His eyes widened.

"My, oh my," he murmured audibly enough for her to hear. "The Lord *does* work in mysterious ways."

The sun was beginning to set over the trees lining the soccer field. Judith was late picking Elizabeth up from practice and she was hoping she hadn't had to wait long in the cold. When she arrived, the team was still practicing, so she took a seat on the bleachers and waited. With a tournament coming up, the coaches were pushing the practices to the limit, and that meant until the sun went down, and the players and coaches couldn't see each other in the dark.

As the team gathered for a final word of instruction from Gareth MacCauly, a figure caught the corner of Judith's eye. The man was tall, vaguely familiar, and he was coming directly toward her. Her thoughts were scrambled as she tried to put the form properly there at the field. Try as she might, the man and location didn't belong. Mercer! For a moment she struggled to rationalize his presence. He has a daughter here? No daughter. A friend, perhaps? Not with the determined step he was walking toward *her*. There was a sense of dread now. Mercer was paying a personal call on her, and he'd gone out of his way to track her down. Someone at the office must have told him where she'd be.

Instinctively, she remained seated as he stopped at the side of the bleacher.

"Judith. . . ."

She knew she was in trouble already. He'd dropped the irritating "Jude" from his vocabulary. And as she rose to talk to him, he'd taken her elbow and lifted, firmly enough for her to pull her arm back.

". . . I was passing by on my way home . . . I just live a mile or so north of here . . . and I thought I'd come by and chat about the Russell case."

"There's nothing to chat about, Aaron. There was a proceeding this afternoon. You weren't available, so I went down to Presiding."

"And agreed to a continuance."

"Yes. A short one. The judge wouldn't wait for you to appear."

"It's the agreement to continue that I was concerned with. . . ."

"It seemed the thing to do. It was going to be granted anyway."

"Well, I don't want to seem overly anxious, but I wanted to talk about it. It couldn't wait 'til morning."

"Is there something more we need to talk about that can't wait?"

He was not in the least apologetic. Couldn't he see how out of place this was, how inappropriate? If he did, he showed not the slightest evidence of it. Nor did he show any signs of ending the awkward discussion.

"You know how I feel about Larson."

"We all feel about the same way, Aaron, I can. . . ."

A hand reached for Judith's elbow from behind her back.

"Mrs. Thornton, I need to talk with the parents for a moment."

It was Gareth MacCauly.

"There's a meeting?" Judith asked.

He pointed toward the grass mound at the
opposite side of the field.

"Over there."

She stood, Mercer with a hand on one elbow
lecturing her on the niceties of trial protocol.
The soccer coach's hand on her other elbow as
he pointed to a meeting on a grassy mound
with not a single person on it. The three stood
a moment before Mercer spoke.

"I'm not going to keep you, Judith. We can
talk tomorrow."

"Tomorrow, Aaron. I'll be in at seven-
thirty."

Mercer left, jogging back to the parking lot.

"I'm sorry, I didn't introduce you. That was
. . . an attorney from my office . . . Aaron Mercer. He, he needed to talk to me."

MacCauly took his hand from Judith's elbow. "No problem."

She was scrambling to reorient herself.

"I missed a meeting?"

He was matter-of-fact. "There's no meeting,
Mrs. Thornton."

"No meeting? But . . . you just said. . . ."

"It was an emergency."

"I'm sorry, you've lost me."

"It's what some of us coaches call our rescue
meeting. If someone's in need of pulling away

from a bad situation, an angry parent, some such thing, we call a meeting."

"I . . . didn't know I needed rescuing. . . ."

He looked down at the arm that a moment earlier rested firmly in his hand.

"Then why are you shaking so badly, miss?"

Judith's eyes followed his. Her hand was shaking. So was her other hand. And her arms.

"It's cold."

"It is. That it is."

She looked at him and took a deep breath.

"Thank you."

"No need for thanks. Glad to help."

That was the end of the conversation. He turned and walked away toward the clubhouse. She was becoming gradually more aware of the man. He was unusual; his senses quite different than the bookish egos surrounding her most of the day. He'd been too far away to have possibly overheard her conversation with Mercer. Rather, he'd picked up the inflections of her movement and those of Mercer. Had they presented such a melodramatic scene? She wouldn't have thought so. MacCauly seemed to be the only one who noticed them. In a small, growing way, it pleased her.

And Mercer. What reasons could have existed for his tracking her—yes, tracking her, for it couldn't be called anything else—to the field at such a late hour? He said it was the case. But the case could have waited for tomorrow. Pure emotion that had driven him there. What particular emotion it might be, was for the moment not clear to her. It was the first time in the several encounters with Mercer that she could honestly say she'd been afraid of the man.

13

<AT> 7:30 AARON Mercer walked into Judith's office and left a note: "Please call me." That was all it said. She'd told him she would be in at 7:30 and hadn't made it until 7:45. The terseness of the note irritated her. He hadn't addressed it to her by name, although he'd signed his own. It was more a command he'd left for her, the way someone would leave a note for an employee, and one they didn't care for, at that.

Judith sat, fingering the note. Then she slipped it into the wastebasket under her desk. She had no intention of responding. At 8 o'clock Andrea, Mercer's secretary, dropped into her office.

"Mr. Mercer was wondering if you were available."

Judith tried to look and sound as if nothing could have been further from her mind than seeing Mercer. She treated the question nonchalantly. Actually, it was all she'd been thinking about.

"Anytime."

She consciously avoided revealing where at any time she'd be available. If Mercer wanted to see her, he'd have to come to her. And he did.

At 8:15, sooner than Judith expected, Mercer appeared at her office door. Behind him, she saw several secretaries, looking in the direction of Mercer. The subtle melodrama unfolding hadn't been lost on the office staff.

Mercer glanced quickly at his wristwatch.

"Sorry I'm late, Judith."

Again he'd dropped the "Jude" from his salutation. He was expecting her to apologize, say it was *her* lateness that had caused the delayed discussion. But she didn't. Something held her back.

"That's okay, Aaron. I was a few minutes late myself."

Mercer didn't blink an eye. He took a second or two to respond, and when he did, it wasn't quite what she'd expected.

"Care to have a cup of coffee with me, Judith?"

"Noooo . . . I don't think so, Aaron. I have to get a couple of cases off my desk."

"Maybe later, then?"

"Sure. How about ten-thirty?"

She bit her lip. She should have said no and left it at that. Now she'd jumped right back into whatever was on Mercer's mind.

He seemed surprised. "I'll stop back, then."

Judith managed a weak smile.

As soon as he left, Andrea stepped into the doorway of her office.

"Can I get you a cup of coffee, Mrs. Thornton?"

The secretary didn't need to say it. It was a gesture of support, unspoken and subtle, but there.

"No. But thanks, Andrea."

As she turned to leave, Judith called out after her and she quickly returned, this time coming into the office.

"Can you tell Mr. Mercer something's come up and I won't be able to have coffee this morning?"

"Sure. I'd be happy to."

When Andrea left, Judith reached for the phone.

"Larry? I need to talk with you."

Judith knocked on the door to Larry Farrell's office and waited for his voice. She hadn't decided what she was going to tell him. But she needed to let him know right away that she was feeling more and more uncomfortable with Mercer.

"What's up, Judith?"

"Can I sit down? I need to talk to you about Aaron."

"Is there a problem?"

"Why, whatever makes you think that?"

She was sounding sarcastic and hadn't meant to.

"I'm sorry, Larry. It's difficult to describe what's happening. He seems. . . ."

"Edgy?"

"Well, not exactly edgy. . . ."

"Well, what, then?"

She hadn't thought about this, how difficult it was going to be to talk to Farrell about Mercer. How could he possibly understand what she was experiencing, what she'd seen in Mercer recently? How could she say it? "Aaron left me a note saying he wanted to see me"? She could tell him *what* Mercer had done, but not *how* he'd done it, and how he was behaving was the problem.

It came out far more gently than she'd imagined.

"Is Aaron under any stress lately?"

"Actually, yes. It's good of you to pick it up."

This interested her. Here was the explanation she needed. It would explain everything and put the issue back in perspective. It did neither.

"Aaron's name's about to come down for a Superior Court appointment. He's been in to see me about twice a day for this or that reference or case citation he's worked on. I've gotten several calls on his behalf, so I know the network's out there buzzing. He has a considerable amount of support in all the places you'd expect him to."

"I . . . I had no idea. He didn't say anything to me."

"He wouldn't. Your application's still pending out there for the same seat."

"Yes, but it's been pending for a year. I hadn't expected another shot at it."

"Well, I have to admit a couple of the callers have asked which of you would make the better appointment for the seat."

She didn't ask what he'd told the callers.

"I gave you both very high recommendations," he volunteered.

Now she wanted as much information from him as he could give her.

"Have you really noticed he was edgy?"

"I've known Aaron for twenty years. I've never seen him so nervous about anything. He wants this. Very much."

"That probably explains why he was so upset yesterday."

Farrell was curious.

"Upset about what?"

"I covered for him in a case. You remember the Russell case I thought was so weak and Aaron thinks is so strong?"

"Uh-huh. . . ."

"I consented to a two-week continuance to allow new counsel to prepare for the prelim. Aaron actually tracked me down at my daughter's soccer field and . . . was mad about it."

"I suspect he's going to be treading on thin ice in some of the more sensitive cases. He won't want any bad press. No mistakes. And you know Aaron, he doesn't like to let anyone take control of his caseload."

He was making excuses for the man.

"Can you just keep him off my back, Larry? I can understand his excitement, but I really can't accept his pressure on me."

"Look, Judith, I'm sure in a month or two, when the position's filled, you won't be such a threat to him and he'll settle down."

"How am I a threat to him, Larry? The man steals *my* case. He gets mad because I give the defense a two-week continuance to get new counsel on board in a case so weak I suspect there's no case against a man sitting in jail with his family falling apart . . . and I'm a threat to *him*!"

Farrell was letting her go on. He was enjoying watching her get angry.

"Haven't done or said anything to irritate the man."

"Ah, but you have, Judith."

The comment stopped her. "What have I done?"

"Nothing."

"What? Excuse me," she leaned over the desk toward Farrell. "I've missed something here."

"Nothing irritates a man like Aaron more than a nonconfrontational woman. I suspect he's not quite sure how to deal with you."

"He could start by being polite. Genuinely polite." She realized Farrell wouldn't have any idea what she was referring to.

"You're a woman, Judith. And a bright one at that. You're also competing with him for a job he desperately wants."

"So? I can't help either condition."

"Just keep it in mind, that's *all* I'm saying. And if there's anything you need to talk over, come talk to me."

"Are you going to have this same conversation with Aaron? I mean, about trying to keep ourselves civil until the judicial spot's filled?"

"Not unless he wants to talk. Until that time, there's not a lot I can do."

"Well, thanks for the ear, Larry. At least I know where the man's coming from."

Judith left the office calmly, but inside she was seething.

Mercer was near out of control on more than one level. And if Farrell couldn't deal with him, she would. And she'd do it her own way.

At her desk, she stared down at the files she needed to look through for the morning. It was already 10 o'clock. This thing with Mercer was sapping her energy, distracting her. She was angry, but not certain how to handle it now, although it was clear she would have to handle it on her own.

As she worked her way through the morning assignments, Judith became aware of the one-page memo at the bottom of the files. It was a memo from Mercer to Farrell with a copy to her. It was succinctly titled "Update on Russell Case." She scanned it quickly, even though her first impulse was to throw it away. The Russell case wasn't her case. It wasn't assigned to her unit. There was no need to send a copy to her. Only the most cursory review showed the real reason for the memo. After a short summary of the status of the case, the intent was clear.

"Without my consent or knowledge, the matter was continued in court for a period of two weeks by Judith Thornton."

Mercer wanted to take a potshot at her, and he had. And oddly enough, she had a feeling Farrell was irrelevant to Mercer. Farrell couldn't care a fig that Judith had made a call to continue a case for two weeks. The memo was intended for her.

As she set the memo on the desk, wondering what, if any, kind of response was necessary or even possible, a voice called from the doorway.

"Hey, Jude, it's almost ten-thirty. How about some coffee?"

She looked up to see Mercer standing at the door.

"No, Aaron. Thanks. I've still got a lot to do this morning."

"Okay . . . offer still stands. I'll buy, if that makes any difference."

"No. Not really. I just have too much work."

Mercer shook his head slightly and disappeared.

God damn it, Judith, when are you going to level that man?

But she couldn't answer her question.

14

―――◆◆◆―――

"ANNETTE'S GOT PNEUMONIA."

Judith wanted to ask if it was bad, but in Annette's condition it was lethal, and she knew it.

"She took a real turn for the worst."

On the other end of the phone, Annette's sister began to cry.

"She's not responding. She's in and out, you know?"

Judith knew all too well. Annette's condition made her request to Judith all the more imperative.

"I have something I need to talk to you and Mark about. It's important I see you right away—tonight, if we can all get together. I can sit with Annette and give you all a little breather, too."

At home, on Judith's library desk, were the documents incorporating Annette's request. Judith asked her probate attorney to draw up something simple, just something saying Sarah would become Judith's ward if anything happened to Mark. The request could have been more formalized, and indeed, to make the request stick, should have been more formalized. But time was of the essence, and there was something about the situation that Judith realized needed to be kept under control and eased into gently, with everyone understanding this was one of Annette's last wishes. There was no time to battle about the contents or see a judge. She hoped everyone understood the spirit of the document.

The night was cold, crystal clear. Judith's car wound up Soledad Mountain Road, toward a house she'd visited hundreds of times, where her daughter played and spent the night. In the distance, she could see the lights of Chula Vista, and beyond, Tijuana and the black void of the Pacific Ocean.

She parked her car on the street and walked up the sharp incline of a driveway to Annette's house. A woman appeared moments after Judith rang the doorbell and introduced herself as Annette's sister, Helene. Judith stepped into the house and was met by Mark. His face was drawn. Dark circles of fatigue ringed his eyes. He somehow looked shorter.

"Judith," he said softly, "thank you for coming."

"I wanted to see Annette, and Mark, I do need to talk to you and Helene. Is Sarah here?"

He shook his head.

"No, no, in fact, it's better she's not here. Can we sit down just a minute before we go in to see Annette? I really need to get this off my chest.''

Mark showed her into the living room, and he and Helene sat on either side of her on the sofa. It was a configuration of the three, as if both Mark and Helene wanted, needed, to be physically close to her, to anyone who might for a moment or two help share their burden.

Judith pulled a two-page document from the thin brown leather briefcase she'd carried in with her.

''I don't want either of you to think I in any way initiated this. Annette asked me to talk with the two of you and see if I could have a paper drawn up that could assure her you'd let me be Sarah's guardian if Mark dies.''

''Why in God's name would she do a thing like that?'' Helen asked, bewildered.

''I'm at a loss, too,'' Mark added, covering his face with his hands and shaking his head.

''Please,'' Judith said, ''it's just something she got into her mind she wanted. Maybe it's Sarah's friendship with Elizabeth. The important thing is that you'll hopefully never have to reach that issue. What's important is that Annette know it's okay with the two of you.''

Helene began to sob loudly, wiping away the water now soaking her cheeks.

''The doctor says she's not going to last more than two days. How do they know that?''

Judith put her hand on Helene's arm.

''They don't know. But if she's still able to understand you, you have to let her know this is okay. I can't tell you how important it is to her. If she's dying, she needs to know."

Judith was surprised she said it so easily. "She's dying." It was direct. No inflection. No emotion.

"I don't think she understands anything, Judith," Mark said, wiping the tears now streaming down his face. "She's just hanging on. Just hanging on, for what, I don't know."

"Will you sign this? For her?"

"I'll sign. I'll work something out, if we come to that," Helene said.

"It doesn't matter to me anymore," Mark added. "I talked to her about my brother being guardian. She didn't want it and we had an argument about it. But I don't care anymore."

He rose and went into the kitchen, bringing a pen with him. First he, then Helene, signed at the bottom of the second page. They signed quickly, so fast that Judith realized if Mark fell dead at that moment and Annette followed suit, Helen would disregard the promise she'd just made and fight for custody of Sarah. But there was no need for formality or pride. Even though the signing now seemed to her so much a sham, so designed to mollify a dying woman, it was also the right thing to do, and she felt a satisfaction and strength in having brought the situation to this point.

The signatures on the document, Judith asked if she could see Annette. She followed Mark down the hallway to a small bedroom.

Annette, her eyes closed, lay on her back under a thin yellow blanket, her legs straight, her head propped up by two yellow pillows.

"The priest's been here and left. So's the

doctor. All we can do is keep her comfortable," Helene whispered. "The doctor said
she'd linger a long time maybe, but mercifully,
she wouldn't understand anything around
her."

"Well," Judith smiled slightly, "I don't
abide much by the advice of doctors, Helene.
I assume Annette's able to hear and understand exactly what's being said around her.
The first thing we need to do is make her comfortable, though, like the good doctor said."

Judith grabbed several pillows from the
large chair next to the bed and placed them
under Annette's knees.

"I don't know if this works, but my mother
used to think it made her more comfortable.
Why don't you make some tea and relax? I'll
sit with her."

Mark and Helene left quickly, anxious to do
any act that smacked of hospitality or brought
a moment of relief from the waiting. Judith sat
on a small chair next to the head of the bed.
All the feelings returned. The hours she'd sat
with her mother. The non-response from a
woman who you could only hope was comfortable and relieved from pain. Who you
hoped understood the things you said and
wanted to say but could not. But she felt far
more strange about this, sitting next to Annette. She'd been through it, they hadn't.

Annette's hands rested at her sides. Judith
had never noticed how small they were, how
tapered her fingers were. They'd been able to
take fragments of ribbon and turn them into
magnificent bows at Christmas and paint in-

credible scenes. They were the hands of an artist. Judith picked up Annette's hand lying nearest her. And she said it again, the same words almost verbatim that she'd said to her mother. It was remarkable, and yet she needed to say them to Annette, and this time, this time, she knew why she was saying them.

"Annette. It's me, Judith. I know you can hear me. I wanted to tell you everything's the way you wanted it. The document, Mark, Helene. It's all . . . just the way you need it to be. It's all going to be okay."

Judith took both her friend's hands in her own. Something was different, though. And it struck her suddenly. One of Annette's hands was much cooler than the other. She'd have to be careful! She'd once called the hospice nurse when her mother's feet were cold because the doctor said cold feet could be a symptom of the body starting to shut down. She'd been wrong and had looked foolish when the nurse had rushed to the house only to tell Judith her mother needed another cover to keep her feet warm. She'd felt so inept, then so embarrassed.

She held each of Annette's hands separately. There could be no mistake. The left hand was cooler than the right.

Mark and Helene appeared together, Helene carrying a tray with a cup of tea, and a sugar bowl and spoon. She was smiling, and Judith felt good that there was a moment of lightness that seemed to settle over them. She was happy she'd helped create that moment. She sat with them for an hour, talking about Elizabeth and Sarah, little things she'd done with Annette, their shopping trips. Then she rose to leave, promising to return and visit the next evening.

"Mark, can you walk to the car with me?" she asked.

As soon as they reached halfway down the driveway, Judith turned to him.

"Mark, one of her hands is markedly cooler than the other. Check it when you go back. With my mother they said it was a sign her system might be shutting down and she could go quickly if that happened. Please, I don't want to alarm anyone, I'm probably wrong. I've been wrong about it before. But bring Sarah home tonight, please. I just don't know. This is different. I feel like she should be here with Annette tonight. Mark?"

"Of course I will, I will, Judith."

"Mark. Promise me you'll bring Sarah home. And stay close to Annette. Call the doctor and ask him about what I said." She took a few steps and stopped. "You know, Mark, if I'd just given my mother a hug good-bye the day she died, maybe I'd have seen the physical signs and been able to be with her. She died by herself. I'll always live with that, always regret it. Don't let it happen to you."

"I won't, Judith. I promise." He bent forward and kissed her lightly on the cheek. "Please try to come tomorrow."

The phone rang at 6:30 the next morning. It was Annette's sister.

The message was simple, mingled with

tears. Annette had died the night before. Mark and Sarah were with her. And before she died, she'd opened her eyes and looked at them, and they thought she'd smiled.

"Thank you, Judith. Mark says to thank you."

15

SAINT AUGUSTINE WAS a small church, humble in comparison with the larger Catholic churches in the city. Annette's funeral service was scheduled there for 10:30 A.M. the Monday following her death. Because it was a weekday, Judith had arranged to have one of Elizabeth's friends who was attending the service pick Elizabeth up from school and take her along. Judith went in to her office and left early, promising Elizabeth to meet her there.

Elizabeth was nervous. This would be her first funeral. Judith hadn't required she attend, but the girl had insisted. Other friends of Sarah's would be there. She needed to be there, too.

Parking was a problem. The narrow streets of San Diego could accommodate some of the overflow from the church, but most, including Judith, had to park their cars on the side streets several blocks away. By the time Judith arrived at the church doors, a crowd spilled from the small church onto the front steps. They stood shoulder to shoulder, not giving an inch, listening to the priest as best they could.

Judith's height wasn't helping. She could barely see through the shoulders of several of the taller men standing in front of her. The women wearing hats took care of the rest of her view, reducing it to snatches of visibility available only when someone shifted position.

Straining, Judith spotted Elizabeth standing against the wall at the front of the church. Next to her were the friends she'd come with. Elizabeth was unable to see her mother, stretching her neck periodically, moving her head in every direction, hoping she'd arrived.

How to get to her? Judith could feel her frustration level rising. No one was moving. She'd have to wait the entire service. That could take an hour. She pressed against the woman standing in front of her. *If I move forward, maybe she'll step to the side, and open it up.* She pushed but the woman didn't budge. *Don't dive in. Wait for any movement and flow with it. Wait for something to happen.* Where had she heard that? At soccer. The coach was telling a player not to jump at the opponent with the ball . . . wait for the mistake, the opportunity to strike. She waited. She could hear the priest urging people forward now. The communion.

A line formed in the center aisle of the church as people waited to take communion. Then came the warning, a gentle reminder that only those who practiced the Catholic faith should be stepping in to take the wine and wafer.

The man and woman standing directly in front of Judith moved. She, without thinking, announced, "Excuse me. Excuse me, please. I need to take communion."

The people in front of her, as if in command from a higher authority, parted, and Judith stepped through, into the church. There was no way to go but forward, to the priest. She looked, but there were no seats to her right or left, and sitting was of no use, anyway. She was trying to reach Elizabeth, who, having spotted her mother advancing, took on a puzzled look. Neither was Catholic.

Inch by inch she neared the priest. A fear arose. It might be considered a sin to take communion like this if you weren't Catholic. She'd been told not to. But if communion was good for the soul, why should God care if you were or weren't Catholic? Rationalization aside, it wasn't the taking of communion that was a falsity, it was the motive, the fact of the matter was, she was using it to get from one place to another.

Her turn. Face to face with the priest. A piece of a wafer. A sip of wine from a glass, and then, on impulse, she made the sign of the cross. The priest's eyes widened just enough for her to realize she'd made an Orthodox cross, not the sign of the cross used by the Catholic Church.

Judith hurried past the front row, bending to shake hands with Annette's family, who reached out to her. Then she was at Elizabeth's side, her arm around the girl's shoulder, avoiding the sideways glance of the priest, as he gave the last of the communion.

Annette would have been amused. And in a strange, odd way, she was pleased with herself, but without knowing quite why. It was not the proper thing to do. Not something she would have done a month ago.

16

"RUSSELL'S IN THE county hospital, Mr. Larson."

Alan Larson had waited patiently for the heavy metal door to open and his new client to appear; waiting for a chance to interview Thomas Russell, talk to him in detail about the night his daughter was assaulted. It was one of the expectations that trial counsel would have a report or personal notes at least of his client's account of the events surrounding his arrest. No such report was contained in Travis Fuller's file. There were some sketchy notes, one- and two-word phrases that seemed to give an account of the evening Caryn was assaulted. But what was lacking was an in-depth account by the defendant himself. Larson wanted to start with such an account, wanted to look Thomas Russell in the eye and ask him what had happened.

Instead of being greeted by his client, the duty sheriff who should have been escorting the man came into the interview room alone and announced that Thomas Russell had been hospitalized.

"With what?" Larson asked.

"With an acute case of attempted suicide."

Depression, even attempts at one's life, were not unusual in jail. Larson began packing up the papers and police reports he'd spread across the interview table.

"When'd it happen?"

"This morning. Early. About four-thirty, we guess. Tried to hang himself from one of the bars on the door to his cell. Used his pants to do it. Didn't work. Pants were too thick to pinch off the air and the cell bars aren't high enough. But I'd say he made his point."

"Yeah, I'd say so, too. What kind of condition was he in when he was sent to County?"

"I saw him. He looked okay to me. A little white, maybe. A little in shock. But it was pretty clear he was going to live, you know?"

"Thanks. I think I'll head down to the hospital and see if I can talk with him."

"No need. I got word he's on his way back already. All they did was check him over and give him a new seal of approval. And oh, Larson, you might be interested to know when they first pulled him down, he was mumbling something like, "I couldn't have" or "How could I have?" . . . words to that effect. It all got written down in the report that got filed. Interesting words, huh?"

Larson didn't respond. His client was a innocent man. An honorable defendant. He'd have liked to have kept it that way, but this attempted suicide and the words, they'd be used against him. They weren't a confession, but they and the act of suicide itself could be admissions, comments leading a reasonable person to believe that he was guilty.

"When do you figure he'll be available for me?'

The deputy looked at his watch.

"Maybe an hour. Maybe an hour and a half."

Larson had no intention of hanging around the jail for that long a period of time. He pulled his briefcase from the desk.

"You comin' back, Larson?"

Alan Larson didn't respond. An hour and a half was about what it would take to drive over to the Russell house and see if Marilyn Russell could talk to him. At his car, he used his cell phone. She was in and yes, he could come over.

17

ALAN LARSON DIDN'T know what to expect when he rang the doorbell at the Russell home. His telephone conversation with Marilyn Russell had been only a few minutes. She knew of her husband's suicide attempt and didn't want to talk about it over the phone. He could understand her desire to wait on the subject, but there was, he detected, a certain calm in her voice that he would not have expected from a wife whose husband had tried to take his life the night before. He was anxious to see what physical reactions awaited him at the house.

It took a full minute for Marilyn Russell to answer the doorbell. Larson wondered if the woman had left, even knowing he was then on his way to talk to her. His concern, however, about the effects of her husband's attempt on his life was allayed somewhat when the door opened wide. The lids of her eyes were swollen, the whites red.

"Mr. Larson. Come in." Her voice was off, yet there was that firmness, that matter-of-fact inflection he'd heard in her and in their earlier conversation. "I just called the hospital and they told me Tom's going to be fine. He tried to hang himself from one of the vertical bars. No small feat. It was probably doomed to fail from the start. He's got some bruising around his neck. The jail guards caught him before he could really hurt himself. They said the pants were too thick to break his neck, but it could've choked off the oxygen if he'd hung there a long time." She turned directly to Larson. "Oh, I'm sorry, Mr. Larson, you probably already know all this."

"No, I don't. Can I call you Marilyn?"

"I don't mind."

"Call me Alan, too. I don't much care about formality with my clients. Actually, I haven't talked with your husband yet. What he did was the act of a man who's getting desperate. My concern is that he made some statements after he was freed from the bar. Statements to the effect he was sorry. Sorry for what? That's what the jury's going to ask if we get that far. Was he saying he was sorry for what he did to his daughter?"

"Can I get you some coffee, Alan?"

"I'd love some, thanks."

Larson followed her into the small kitchen and watched her pour two cups of coffee from the white Corning ware coffeepot on the stove. The kitchen, like the other rooms he could see in the house, was small. Cupboards thick with layers of white paint lined two of the walls. The remaining walls were painted a bright yellow. He guessed the house was built in the forties, maybe just after the war.

Marilyn carried the cups and several spoons to the small round wood table next to a window overlooking the backyard.

"Cream and sugar's here on the table. Caryn's outside."

She nodded her head in the direction of a swing set in the far right corner of the yard. The girl was sitting in a swing, alone, dragging the toe of her shoe in the dirt as she drifted gently back and forth over the large rut under her.

"She looks sad, doesn't she, Alan?" Marilyn Russell spoke without taking her eyes off her daughter.

Larson was watching Marilyn Russell carefully. She was detached, almost talking to herself. "She has plenty of reason to be sad," he added.

"She's a quiet kid. A good student. She doesn't deserve this."

"None of you deserve this, Marilyn. But I need some information, because things just got a little tougher for me this morning. The statements your husband made might be taken as admissions of some kind. An apology for something he might have done. Like assaulting Caryn."

"He wasn't talking about Caryn. He was talking about him and me." She stopped, the void filled with the metallic ping of her spoon hitting the sides of the china cup as she stirred her coffee.

"Is there something happening between the two of you?"

She stopped stirring her coffee and set the spoon down next to the sugar bowl.

"I saw Tom yesterday at the jail. And I told him something I'd been thinking about for awhile. I told him I wanted a separation. A legal separation."

"I, I don't understand. . . ."

"Come with me, Mr. Larson." She pushed her chair from the table and picked up her coffee cup, carrying it with her. Larson did the same.

She led him through a small hallway to a bedroom, obviously Caryn's. Yellow gingham covered the bed and framed the large window, the window she'd insisted a man had come through to attack her.

Marilyn Russell pointed toward the bed. "There used to be a picture of Tom there, by Caryn's bed. She's put it away somewhere. She doesn't talk about her father anymore. Doesn't ask when he's coming home. How he is. She did. Before the interviews with the investigators. And the psychological testing. Before the pressure and the finger pointing. I don't know what she believes anymore. I don't know if she even still thinks her father's innocent. How could she, with so many people telling her, implying to her that it really was her father? A kid gets confused with all that. And then there's everything else. This little house is all we have. It's mortgaged to the hilt. And the payment's a month behind. I can't concentrate on anything. I sit at work and stare at the desk. I've sat there for hours, sometimes, not knowing what to do, losing track of time. I used to love this house, Mr. Larson. Now I hate it. I hate coming home at night."

"So you told this to Tom?"

"Not exactly the way I just told you, but in so many words, yes, I did. Because Caryn can't take much more of this. I can't, either. Nothing's ever going to be the way it was. Ever again. Even if the person who really did it was caught tonight and Tom came home tomorrow. All those shrinks Caryn's seen would have to create some kind of miracle to put my family all back together again. I don't think they can. There's been too much pain. Too much damage. I told him I wanted a legal separation. When this is over I'm taking Caryn out of here. To my sister's in Oregon. We can deal with it from there."

"You told this to Tom? That you were leaving him."

"Uh-huh . . . I did. And he just stared at me. He didn't say 'No, please don't do that.' He just stared at me awhile, then got up and left the visiting area. I tried to get him to come back, talk about it. But he wouldn't come back. That was the last time I saw him or talked with him before he did this thing last night. I wish. . . ." Her last statement drifted.

"You wish what?"

She turned to him, her jaw set, a strange, cold look in her eyes. "I wish . . . I wish he'd have been successful, Mr. Larson. I wish he'd killed himself. Then we'd all be free from this hell. Do you think I'm a bad person for feeling that way, Alan?"

"Marilyn, you're talking like a woman who's given up. Don't do that. There's help. I can get some counseling for the family. You can make it work."

"Oh, can I, Mr. Larson?" Hers was a sarcastic tone tinged with a bitterness, perhaps even anger. "I want to show you this."

Her pace quickened from the doorway of Caryn's bedroom back to the kitchen, and a small floor to ceiling broom closet. She pulled the door of the closet open from its spring hinge. Inside were several brooms.

"On the night Caryn was attacked, I got up. I don't know why. It was about three-thirty. Tom wasn't in bed. I went downstairs and found him sleeping on the sofa in the den. The television wasn't on. He'd been drinking, Mr. Larson. Heavily. He'd been promising me he would stop. I thought he'd done that. What I didn't know was that he still had a bottle of bourbon here, in the closet."

"Are you telling me your husband was drunk the night Caryn was attacked?"

"I found him down here. Out cold. He's been to AA meetings to try to stop. For almost a year now. I thought he was making progress. I believed in him, Mr. Larson. I. . . ." She put her hand over her mouth as if trying to stop herself from saying what she was about to say. Instead, it stifled the sob she was trying to choke back. "I don't believe in him anymore. Worse than that, I don't know if he even remembers what happened the night Caryn was hurt. He was drunk. Dead drunk. Passed out on the sofa while his daughter was being attacked upstairs, or. . . ."

She didn't need to finish the sentence. She doubted her husband's innocence.

"I don't want to know the truth of this, Mr. Larson. I just want to leave before I lose my daughter, my house, my mind, everything."

Larson could think of nothing else to say. Russell's act of despondency was explainable now, and as horrible as it was, at least it wasn't directly tied to guilt, but rather the announcement by his wife that their marriage was over. It might actually work to his benefit. It might be a plus in his defense.

"Mrs. Russell, can I talk to Caryn?"

"I don't mind, but. . . ."

"No, don't worry. I won't confuse her any more than she's been confused already. I need to talk to her about her testimony."

"Do you want me to call her in?"

"No. I'll sit outside with her. I think that'll be a lot less threatening."

Larson pushed open the screen door to the back porch. The door squeaked open and banged shut behind him. He stood on the cement slab and stepped down the two concrete steps onto the grass. Caryn had noticed his presence immediately. Bringing her swing to a stop, she watched the man walk across the yard to where she sat.

"Hi, Caryn." Larson leaned on the edge of the brick planter next to the swing set. "My name's Alan Larson. You can call me Alan, if you want. Your mom's just inside the kitchen there. She said it would be okay to talk with you. I'm the person who's going to defend your dad in court. I'm his lawyer."

"What happened to Mr. Fuller? Isn't he going to be the attorney anymore?

"No, he's not, Caryn. I'm taking his place."

"He didn't believe my dad."

"How do you know that, Caryn?"

The girl shrugged her shoulders and looked at the ground.

"Because he never told me he believed him. Like I believed him."

Larson knew the reasons Fuller could never vocalize his personal beliefs. All he'd need was for Mercer to ask her whether anyone had told her that her father wasn't guilty. She'd say, "Sure, my dad's lawyer told me he wasn't guilty." And that would be the end of her credibility. It was too complicated a trial maneuver to explain to a child.

"Well, Caryn, we lawyers like to just get your views, you know? We don't want to try to make you say something you don't want to say."

She looked up from the dirt into Larson's face.

"Do you think he's guilty?"

Larson didn't hesitate for a moment.

"I believe he is innocent, Caryn. I'm going to do everything I can to get him home as fast as I can. All I need is for people to tell the truth. Do you know what the truth is, Caryn?"

"It's when you don't make things up. You're honest."

"And what happens if you don't tell the truth?"

"You get punished if you lie."

"Will you promise me that you'll only tell the truth?"

"I will."

Larson had accomplished two things at once. He'd won the girl's trust, and he'd started preparing her for her testimony. In order to have a child as young as her testify, the court was going to want to see if she was competent. That meant in part that she knew the difference between true and false statements and that she understood there were punishments for people who lie. As they got closer to the day of the preliminary hearing, he'd find a morning or afternoon a court was vacant, and take her inside to sit in the witness chair and speak into the microphone. For now, he wanted to see what kind of story she'd give him of the night she was attacked.

A half hour later Larson walked into the kitchen to find Marilyn still sitting at the table, a now cold cup of coffee before her.

"She still insists it's not Tom who did it."

"And you believe her?"

"And I believe her."

"I wish I could."

"You will again, Marilyn. Just give me some time. I'd like to see Caryn's room again."

Before he'd finished the sentence, Larson was walking toward the hallway and the girl's bedroom, Marilyn following him. She watched as he stood next to the bed, then walked to the bedroom window. The lock at the top of the window was one of the old turn style that twisted clockwise, the top hinging under the bottom metal portion. Larson ran his hand over it.

"We keep it locked all the time now."

"Was it locked the night Caryn was attacked?"

"I don't know if it was or not."

"Did the police check it when they came out, or ask about it?"

"I don't recall them doing those things, no. But they came into the bedroom and made a report. They were here for some time. At least a couple of hours."

Larson unhinged the window lock and pushed up on the white wood frame. The window opened easily. It was clean on the outside as well as the inside. No dust or dirt.

"Is the window always this clean?" he asked, smiling at the puzzled woman.

"I try. Caryn's got a dust allergy. I get everything scrubbed down at least twice a month."

"Did the window open this well on the night Caryn was attacked?"

"I'm sure it did. No one's worked on it since then."

Larson poked his head outside the window and looked down toward the ground, a distance of perhaps three feet.

"Nothing's changed with the ground level either, right?"

"No, it was right the way you see it now."

"Even the ground down there?

Marilyn stuck her head out the window and

looked down. Beneath the window, the grass was worn away, exposing dirt.

"That's been like that as long as I can remember. It's just a spot that's refused to grow."

"Bear with me, Marilyn. Can you wait right here? I want to check this from outside."

Larson sprinted from the bedroom, appearing moments later outside of the window. He lifted his right leg, trying in vain to step directly into the bedroom. His inability to do so left him stuck awkwardly, one foot on the ground outside, the knee of his other leg resting on the windowsill.

"That's not going to work, Alan," Marilyn said, explaining the obvious.

"I know," Larson puffed, pulling his body through the window and landing on his hands and knees inside. "I don't think this is how Caryn's attacker got in. Stay here."

Larson rose and headed out the bedroom, once again appearing outside the window. This time, he placed his right foot on the windowsill, using it to lift and balance his body as he glided into the bedroom.

"That's how he got in."

"I don't understand, Alan, what difference does it make?"

"None, except take a look at the windowsill."

The windowsill carried a clear partial print of the sole of Larson's shoe. As he brushed it away, he asked, "To your knowledge, did anyone take any photos of the windowsill after Caryn was attacked?"

"I think they did, yes. They were very thorough. I remember a man with a large camera, an evidence something. . . ."

"An evidence technician?"

"Yeah. That's what they called him. He was here awhile, and he did take photos here in the bedroom."

Did the police do any work with what looked like plaster outside the window?"

"They could have, but I didn't see them do anything like that."

"Can I borrow Caryn for a while? I think you'll have to come with me, too."

"Where do you want to go with her, Alan? I don't want to make this any harder on her than it already is."

"I don't want to, either, but I want to have her try to remember where she went the night she was attacked. She says the man who came into her bedroom window took her for a ride and to get some ice cream. The prosecutor's having a tough time with that story. Frankly, it is a little difficult to follow. Maybe not difficult, just outside the usual type of case we see. I want her to show me what happened, not just tell me."

"Okay, if it will help. But you know it was at night and she'd just gotten up, Alan."

"I realize that. I just want to see if she can give me anything else at all."

"I'll call her. But if it's too much for her, you have to promise we'll call this all off."

"I promise."

As Marilyn went to call Caryn inside, Larson looked around the room one last time.

Had he missed anything else? He hadn't seen any notes in his file about photos of plaster casting. Nothing about entrance evidence or even the state of the bedroom window. This wasn't to say it all wasn't there somewhere. It might just have been that Fuller hadn't looked. Or hadn't known where to look.

At the car, Caryn balked. No more than a slight hesitation, but noticeable to Larson. He said nothing, preferring to observe at this point and ask as few questions as possible. It had not escaped his attention that his car was a black Monte Carlo. Probably close in size to what Caryn described as her attacker's car, and it, too, was black. He stated only that Caryn should sit in the front seat and try to point out where she might have been driven the night she was attacked.

"Drive around here, that way." "Take this street and go up that hill." Her directions were simple and at times seemingly aimless. But she was searching, too. He understood that. He took careful note, however, of the street names, should he have to retrace his own drive.

"Stop! There it is, I know that's it!" Caryn yelled, pointing to a small neighborhood park on a corner. It was a grassy area with a swing set, push merry-go-round, and a large cement turtle.

"What is it?" Marilyn yelled back, equally excited, but not knowing quite what she was excited about.

"That's where the man brought me. See the turtle? There it is. Mr. Larson, you believe me, don't you, that that's it?" she pleaded in one string of breathless exclamations. "Stop the car! I'll show you it's the place. The turtle has one eye painted yellow. The other eye isn't painted. I could see that when he was walking with me past it. I could see that!"

"Have you ever been to this park, Marilyn, with Caryn? Or know if anyone taking care of her would bring her here?"

"It's impossible, Alan. I've never been here with her. I can't imagine her coming this far to a park. There'd be no reason."

Larson parked the car across from the park and ran to the playground equipment, stopping directly in front of the turtle, looking it in the eyes. Then he ran back to the car, going to the trunk and opening it. He removed a small camera.

"Marilyn, and Caryn, can you come with me?"

They complied, following him to the turtle.

"I can't take this photo because if we ever had to use it in court, I'd have to take the stand and testify to its authenticity, that I was the person who took it on such and such a date. You can do it. I can call you to explain how and when it was taken. I want you to take a shot of the turtle's face. With both eyes in it, if you can."

Marilyn walked to the front of the cement animal, and a short gasp emitted from her open mouth. There was only one yellow eye. The other eye was unpainted. Either intentionally, or worn away.

"Take it, Marilyn," Larson urged. "Now

take one of the whole turtle from here." He walked five or six feet away, then motioned for her to come stand where he was.

The photograph taken, Larson called Caryn to him. Placing his hands on her shoulders, he bent to talk to her, his face at the level of her own.

"Caryn. This is going to be hard to do, maybe. But you need to look around this park and tell me if anything else looks familiar to you, if you recognize anything else."

The girl turned to her right and pointed to the bank of shrubbery ringing the grass.

"There."

"What about there?" Larson asked as Marilyn's eyes opened wide in horrified recognition of what her daughter was about to say.

"That's where the man attacked me."

Caryn's voice was forceful. Her choice of words deliberate. She said *attacked.* There was no reticence, far more a tone of vindication.

"Can you take us there and show us?"

The girl marched to the shrubbery, Larson and her mother power-walking to keep up with her.

"This is the place. Here, right here."

Marilyn touched the shrubbery, haltingly pushing aside the thick branches.

"Shall I take a picture here, Alan?

"Take as many as you want."

Ten minutes later they were in Larson's car, heading east in the direction Caryn thought they went when they left the park. But another thirty minutes of driving failed to turn up any sign of an ice cream store, or for that matter, anyplace one could buy ice cream in the early morning hours.

Marilyn nodded toward her daughter. "She's falling asleep, Alan. I think she needs to head home."

"Can I trust you to get the photos developed, Marilyn? I need them right away, like tomorrow."

"I'll take them to a one-hour developer tomorrow morning, if that's okay."

"It'll do. I'll call you tomorrow so I can arrange to pick them up. I don't think any prosecution investigator's going to call you. But you're free of course to talk to them, and if they ask, tell them anything, even about what we saw today."

"Do I have to?"

"No. You don't have to."

They drove the rest of the way home in silence, Marilyn wondering how she could have doubted her husband's innocence; Larson wondering where, in all of San Diego, anyone would be able to buy ice cream after midnight and where the police technician reports were.

18

———

IT WAS A routine report, a monthly catalog of the cases disposed of the preceding month. Some were jury verdicts of guilt, but most were guilty pleas taken by plea bargains. Judith didn't usually spend much time on the reports. They all came to her office for review. No action needed to be taken. She'd just examine the numbers, and keep the most serious offenses isolated for additional follow-through if she deemed it warranted.

This afternoon Judith scanned the report quickly. She had several important cases sitting on her desk, ready to be assigned out to attorneys, and had little time for relaxed reading.

The report this month was only four pages. The pleas taken were impressive. Ten major violators, defendants charged with serious offenses involving violence, pleaded guilty to the facts of the complaints filed against them. All received hefty prison sentences. These more egregious violations were listed up front. They were followed by more brief recitations of other, less serious, cases. One of them caught Judith's eye.

The defendant's last name was Whaley. The summary of his offenses was of particular interest: "Prison sentence, eighteen years. Six counts, rape of a minor. Three consolidated cases. Defendant entered minor victims' bedroom windows. In all but one case, removed victims from house. Molestations occurred in park. Victims returned home."

Judith reached for the phone and dialed the extension for the records department.

Less than thirty minutes later, a records clerk knocked at Judith's door and entered holding three thick manila-colored files, each labeled in thick black pen "Arthur Whaley." She spread the files side by side and opened the first one to find a booking photograph of Whaley staring up at her. It was a three-by-five glossy black-and-white. She glanced at the summary of personal information under the photo. He was thirty-five, but looked much older. His dark hair was unkempt and dirty; his face was rough, pockmarked with acne. One eye was slightly off-center. He generally fit the description Caryn had given of her attacker.

Judith searched for and found the envelope, marked *confidential*, which held the probation report. It would contain a concise summary of Whaley's background and criminal record and the facts of the case. The information in the six-page report was of even greater interest than the appearance of the defendant. The victim in the case had been six years old. Whaley admitted having staked out the victim's house for several days when he was in the neighborhood visiting friends. He'd even conversed with the victim on several occasions. On a Friday night, after drinking several beers, he'd opened the downstairs window of the victim's house, crawled through it, and carried the victim outside. He admitted threatening the girl if she yelled out and threatening to kill her family. After driving the child around for a short period of time, he took her to a park not far from her house, where he molested her. Then he returned to her home and helped the girl back through the window, again threatening to return to kill her parents if she told on him.

The similarity to the Russell case was incredible. Judith quickly examined the remaining Whaley files and found them remarkably similar. Same MO. Same sexual attack in a park with a return to the victims' homes.

Judith's heart was beating faster by the time she'd finished reviewing the files. The question eating away at her, though, was, where had the victims lived? She jotted the street addresses down and walked to the office library to retrieve a street map of San Diego.

One by one Judith pinpointed the location of the victims' homes. All were within three miles of each other. Where did they live in relation to the Russells?

Judith reached for the phone again. Again she directed the records office to retrieve a case, this one the Russell file. Ten minutes later her phone buzzed. It was the records clerk, reporting what she should have known already, that the Russell file was still in Aaron Mercer's office.

Judith took a deep breath. She wanted Aaron to hand over the Russell file so she could compare it to the Whaley offenses on the desk in front of her.

19

"I'M SORRY, JUDITH, but the file's at home.
I've been working on it there in the evenings."

Judith hadn't relished going to Mercer to
ask for the Russell file, not with his sensitivity
to her interest in the case. Better, she thought,
to just tell him what was behind the request
and then deal with whatever fallout there was
from it.

Mercer was sitting at his desk, preparing
what appeared to be a draft of a charging document. He wrote while she talked, appearing
too busy to stop and chat. Judith positioned
herself directly in front of his desk. He would
have to look up at her when, if, he decided to
respond to what she was about to say.

"Why would you want to see it, anyway?"

"I want to be candid with you, Aaron. I was
reading through the monthly summary of
cases disposed of, and I saw a defendant
whose crimes closely matched the one Tom
Russell's charged with." He looked up at her,
his eyes narrowing. "It's a defendant who
came through the bedroom window of his vic-

tims, took them outside to a park, where he assaulted them, and brought them back home again. That's such a close match with the Russell case that I think we need to take a look at the specifics of them and the attack on Caryn Russell.''

Mercer pushed his chair back from the edge of his desk and rubbed the palms of his hands together as if they were cold and he was warming them.

''You know as well as I do, Judith, that any case similar to one being prosecuted is irrelevant. I know you're aware of that because I've seen you resist the use of other crimes' evidence more than once. And very effectively, too, I might say. What some other defendant did isn't relevant to whether our defendant did what he's charged with. I haven't any interest in examining other crimes, no matter how similar they are to the Russell case. And I hope it's not your intention to start working on a case that's not yours. I don't want to seem ungrateful. I appreciate the help. But I also think it's hard for two people to be working on the same case and the same issues. I'm sure you'd agree with that.''

''Generally, I do Aaron. But Caryn Russell's story is so strange, I mean about the man taking her from her bedroom. Buying her ice cream, then returning her home. If this has happened in other cases, especially if it happened near the Russell house, we ought to look at it. Not from a viewpoint of whether or not it's going to be used at trial, but to see whether the man ought to be charged with something in the first place that could have been committed by someone else. It's still very early in the process here. It's just basic fairness."

For a moment, Mercer was tempted to tell her he'd already considered the cases against Whaley, but he decided against it.

"I'm sorry, Judith. I don't think the Whaley case is relevant. I'm moving forward with the case against Russell. He's got a few more days to prepare, and I'm hoping he'll enter a plea so I don't have to put his daughter on the stand to testify against him about what happened to her the night she was attacked."

"Have you given Russell the standard conditions on the plea?"

"I sure have. After she's put on the stand at the preliminary hearing and there's a bind-over, there *is* no plea. We go to trial."

"Aaron, I have a proposition for you. Why not let me take a look at the Whaley cases? You don't have to mess with them at all. I'll see what's there, if anything. If there's something interesting, I'll let you know. It's a no-risk proposition for you."

Mercer stared at her and shook his head. "No. No, thanks. I really don't need the help, Judith. I'm going to have my hands full with Russell's new attorney, and one of the biggest bargaining chips I've got is the plea being available before, but not after, the preliminary hearing. I'd prefer not to have to deal with the "some other dude did it" defense, especially not from our own office."

"But it hasn't anything to do with winning

the case, Aaron, it has to do with. . . ."

He stood up and finished the sentence for her, ". . . With honor. Yes, I know, Judith. But it's a matter of putting a case together against Alan Larson, too. Why don't you let me handle the case I've been assigned?"

"Larson's got the case?"

"Yes, your favorite."

"'He'll find the Whaley case, Aaron. You're going to have to deal with it."

"Well, if he does, he does. I'll deal with it then, the same way I'm dealing with it now— and that's not to deal with it. It's *irrelevant*. Now, if you'll excuse me, Judith, I'm going out for a sandwich. Care to join me?"

The question was silly. She never had lunch with Mercer; they had nothing in common. She declined and headed back to her office. There was no way Aaron Mercer was going to allow her to touch his case. She could understand his feelings. But she disagreed so strongly with him. It wasn't proper protocol for her to meddle. It wasn't her case, wasn't her responsibility. The risks were great that she'd only be causing a fellow prosecutor grief, perhaps even destroying his case. Every instinct, every shred of experience, told her to stay out of it.

Yet she couldn't. Even if she was risking the wrath of Lawrence Farrell himself, she couldn't keep her hands off this one.

20

THE SOLUTION, WHILE exceedingly underhanded, was simple. Mercer had a hold on the Russell file. He wasn't going to allow Judith to suggest the course of that case, let alone hand the file over to her to examine. But he didn't have the Whaley files any longer. He'd said it himself. He had no use for them. As far as he was concerned, they weren't relevant to the Russell case. But they *were* relevant to Judith. Even if she couldn't connect Russell to Whaley, there was nothing keeping her from connecting Whaley to Russell. Nothing, perhaps, except her ethics.

What she was milling over wasn't legally unethical. Parallel investigations went on all the time. Someone had a case that someone else had a collateral matter in. Would she appreciate it if the tables were turned, if Mercer decided to investigate her defendant for other crimes without telling her? It wasn't done. At the least, it was way beyond the protocol of any prosecuting office. The question was, how far was she willing to go? How close to the edge was she willing to skate before someone stopped her? Was she willing to risk the result? It would mean humiliation, maybe reprimand, maybe more. For the moment, she needn't reach those questions, though they loomed above the horizon, waiting to crush her if she made the wrong decision. For now she needed a good, intense look at Russell and Whaley.

In a matter of minutes, Judith had the Whaley case numbers on her computer. Within the hour, his case files were on her desk, and, pencil in hand, she set out to meticulously summarize the facts of each case and list the similarities to the Russell case. And similar they were. Caryn's description of the marks on her assailant's face matched Whaley's acne scars. The mode of entry into the houses of the victims, through bedroom windows, was identical. The return of the victims to their houses occurred in all but one of the cases. The victims' ages were within a year of each other. And finally, there was the location of the crimes. Judith pulled the city map from her desk drawer and plotted the victims' residences. One by one she circled the streets. They were all within a several-mile radius. Any experienced prosecutor could see the overwhelming similarities. Any experienced prosecutor would have thoroughly investigated Whaley's possible connection to the attack on Caryn Russell. There was no explanation for Mercer's dogged determination to proceed against Russell in the face of the Whaley cases.

Judith considered confronting Mercer directly, or perhaps taking her concerns to Lawrence Farrell. But they'd already told her the Russell case was no longer hers. Therein, of course, lay her course of action. As the head of the Major Violator Unit, she was free to initiate independent investigations into crimes. While the power to do so wasn't unfettered, it was there, at her discretion. Now what she had to do was maneuver the players into the necessary positions.

Judith reached for the phone and dialed a familiar number. After only two rings a gruff voice answered.

"Martin."

Judith hadn't worked with Pike Martin for months. The surly investigator for the San Diego Police Department dropped by occasionally to say hello to her when he was in the building, but the last time he'd been through the building she was in the east, at her mother's funeral, and he'd just left a note of condolence.

"Pike! Judith here."

"Jeez, Judith! It's good to hear from you." His voice lowered. "I was sorry about your mother."

"Thanks, Pike. I really appreciated your note."

"What's up? You got a case?"

"Actually, I do, Pike. It's a kind of interesting one. The guy was charged with three assaults on children—all girls. Same MO. He's pleaded guilty and is in prison, already serving what'll probably be the rest of his life."

Behind the laughter was a gentle sarcasm. "So, my God, woman, what's the case? Sounds to me like you've got your man already put away."

"It's not that easy, Pike. I think he's committed a crime someone else is charged with."

There was a short silence before he said what she expected he would say.

"I don't understand. Why don't you just not prosecute the man you think didn't do it? The system's gotten pretty screwy, Judith, but I didn't think it was so bad you all couldn't pull that one off."

"Because Aaron Mercer's prosecuting the guy I think didn't do it."

Pike uttered a knowing "Oh . . ." then added, "You've talked with Mercer, I assume."

"He won't even let me look at the guy's file."

"You know what you're getting into here, Judith?

"He's not letting go of his defendant. I've looked at the . . . it's a long story, Pike. Nothing's set in concrete yet. I'm just looking at it. But I need your help. The man I think committed the crime's in prison. I need some investigative services. And some of your time."

"Lunch or breakfast?"

"Dinner."

"That much of my time?"

"That much. Maybe more, Pike. And Pike. . . ."

"Yeah?"

"I need to warn you, this one may get

bumpy. Internally bumpy. I'm not on Mercer's favored list right now. If he found out what I was up to, it might mean a lot of heat. You might get singed along with me."

"Singed? Hell, Judith, if . . . no, *when* . . . Mercer finds out you've committed this insult, he's going to try to squash you like a bug."

"I know . . . I know. I'll have to live with that if I decide to go forward with . . . well, I'm not sure what . . . but *something*."

"Let's talk, Judith. I must say, I'm intrigued. In all the time I've worked with you, I don't think I've ever seen you willing to take on the likes of Mercer. You know how I feel about you, Judith. You're about the best I've ever worked with. I wouldn't want to see you do something stupid and throw away all my confidence in you now. Maybe I can talk you out of this."

"It's not going to be easy to do that, Pike."

"How about tomorrow? China Camp at four o'clock?"

"I'll see you then, Pike."

"Judith?"

"Uh-huh. . . . ?"

"Bring whatever files you've got."

She hung up the receiver and buried her face in her hands. Pike needn't have told her how dangerous her course of action was. She was interfering with a colleague's case without telling him.

She was putting her career on the line.

21

AARON MERCER WAS fumbling with the telephone. The new office-office-wide, top-of-the-line executive system that had been installed wasn't working properly. He'd been trying for days to master the call recording device, to no avail.

Mercer carefully pushed the VoiceNet button and listened for the mechanical voice at the other end.

"Welcome to VoiceNet. Please press your ten-digit personal identification number and the pound sign."

Mercer's index finger punched out 8-6-3-3-3-3-1-8-3-3-#.

"Please select from the following menu."

Mercer waited patiently until the voice told him he could press "star- 56" to record. It continued, "You must press an eight followed by the pound sign to stop the recording." He pressed the star, then 5-6.

"Welcome to VoiceNet Conference Recording. You may begin recording for up to fifteen minutes after the signal." This was followed by a short buzz that ended abruptly.

"Testing ... testing ... this is Aaron Mercer. It is now 11:30 on. ..."

A gentle tapping at his office door caused Mercer to stop speaking. He hit the 8 and set the receiver next to the phone.

He yelled, "Come in," and the door opened. Martha Salinger stepped into his office clutching a six-inch-thick transcript to her chest.

Martha Salinger was a bright, ambitious attorney who'd joined the district attorney's office the previous year. Twenty-four, and fresh out of law school, she planned to spend several years honing her trial techniques, then move on to a prestigious civil law firm. And the office was pleased to help her. She had the talent. And she had the looks. Tall, dark brown hair with softer highlighted curls framed her face. She wore St. John's knits. She made the kind of impression the court watchers commented favorably on, and large firms wanted and needed to keep clients happy. In office parlance, she was a "short timer," who pretty much held her own caseload as well as helping wherever, whenever, she was needed. And this morning she'd received a message from Aaron Mercer that he needed her views on a certain rape case he'd been thinking of assigning to her. The transcripts from the preliminary hearing had been delivered to her earlier in the day with instructions to read the victim's testimony carefully. Mercer, it seemed, wanted her personal reaction to the truth and veracity of the victim "for purposes of gauging her believability at trial."

"Martha, please come in and have a seat."

Mercer pointed her toward the chair opposite his desk.

"I assume that's the Mahogany Diaz testimony?"

The woman nodded.

"I've read it all and I believe her. In fact, I think she'll make a great witness."

Mercer shook his head and sat in his desk chair opposite her.

"I'm not as certain as you are. What did you think about her comment that she couldn't feel his prick in her vagina?"

The girl's face flushed beet red. Even seasoned prosecutors had difficulty with the coarse language often solicited at trial. They tried to finesse most graphic visuals and verbal descriptions so the jury got the point without being horribly embarrassed, and, even more important, without making the prosecutor appear downright crude. Mercer's question was totally out of line.

"Great," he replied. "I'm not sure when I can get back to this, but we can find some time in the morning. I'll call you. And why not leave that transcript here with me?"

Martha Salinger laid the heavy book of testimony on the desk and left. Outside the office door she breathed a sigh of relief. That was twice now in the last month she'd been through this with Mercer.

At his desk, Mercer made a note to himself: "Send Mahogany Diaz transcript to Celeste

Armstrong for her reactions to victim's testimony."

He didn't hear the click of his VoiceNet Conference Recorder as it ran out of its fifteen minutes of tape.

22

THE DAY SEEMED to be speeding past Judith. It was already 1 P.M., and she'd be meeting with Pike in several hours. After her conversation with him the day before, she'd assembled the Whaley files and her own notes on the Russell case, taken before her mother's death, when the case was still assigned to her. For good measure, she'd added a map of the city in order to show Pike the proximity of the offenses. She knew Pike would be loath to proceed with a criminal action contrary to another deputy's interests. Granted, he had wandered at times across the bounds of ethical propriety. But each time it had been due to his impatience with the justice system. And each time it had been to catch a criminal. To her knowledge, Pike would never purposely interfere with an ongoing investigation. And that's exactly what she'd be asking him to do.

At lunch, Judith walked to the building cafeteria for coffee. It was one of those patented San Diego days outside, with large, billowy white clouds moving swiftly against blue sky.

She should have been out walking and lamented her lack of motivation. The only time she seemed to get outside in the sun anymore was during Elizabeth's soccer practices and games. Tomorrow there was a practice scheduled in La Jolla and she'd promised Elizabeth she'd stay and watch. She'd begun to actually look forward to it.

As Judith poured cream into the heavy white coffee mug, a familiar voice called to her from the nearby cashier's register. It was Andrea Bracken, Aaron Mercer's secretary, asking if Judith was going to be in during the afternoon. She responded affirmatively and thought nothing more of the brief conversation until Andrea dropped into her office an hour later.

"I brought this for you, Mrs. Thornton. I think you'll find it as interesting as the transcripts you asked for." As she spoke, she handed Judith a small white envelope, which she opened in the secretary's presence. Inside was a cassette tape.

"I don't understand. What's this?" Judith asked.

"It's a tape I pulled out of his VoiceNet Recorder."

"Wait a minute . . . wait a minute. Who are you talking about, Andrea?"

"Mercer. He's been doing this right along. This time, though, he's blown it. He called Martha Salinger into his office and . . . well, you won't believe the things he said to her. I don't know how she took his comments, but I think they're salacious and extremely improper."

"How'd you get this tape? You know it's illegal to tape record a person in California without telling them first."

"Don't worry," the woman said, a hint of defiance in her voice. "He taped himself. He asked me to check the phone because he's having such a hard time learning how to operate it and there on his recorder is that." She stabbed a finger toward the envelope. "He forgot to press the pound sign and it just kept recording. For the heck of it I played it back. It made me blush just listening to it. I can't imagine what that poor woman felt like, having to listen to him."

Judith took out her small office-issued recorder and placed the tape in it.

"I'd put that on real low, Mrs. Thornton. And I'd close the door, if I were you. I don't care to hear it all over again. I'll close the door for you on my way out."

Judith called after her. "Don't you want the tape back?"

She turned and whispered back to Judith. "No. It's a present. Just get that bastard, will you?"

When the secretary left, Judith took earphones from her desk and plugged them into the tape recorder. As she listened, she could feel her face burning. This was far worse than anything she'd witnessed or been subjected to by him.

Now, quite aside from her concerns about Mercer's prosecution of a man who was likely innocent of the crime he was charged with, her concerns over the treatment of Martha Salinger demanded some kind of action, and clearly that action had to start with a discussion of the tape with Martha Salinger.

Martha Salinger's office was county issued, the austere furniture testament to the saying, "It's prison-made." It was. The file cabinet in the corner was gray metal. Yet the junior deputy managed to add elegance to it. The weekend before she'd moved into the office she'd come in and painted it a soft creamy yellow, erasing the county's military green walls. She'd added a pink and mint green oriental rug under the desk and kept a picture-perfect mixture of fresh flowers laced with green fern at the corner of her desk.

As much as Judith liked Martha, she always felt a twinge of uneasiness in the office, could never quite bring herself to just automatically sit down as one colleague did in the office of another. As good an attorney as Martha was, it was a statement Martha Salinger didn't quite belong in the government employ.

"Martha, can we talk about Aaron?" Judith asked, standing before the woman's desk.

Judith wasn't sure how she was going to start the conversation. She'd watched Martha Salinger for any hint of stress or unhappiness. But the woman showed no sign of worry or anxiety. Finally, she decided to simply confront her with her own knowledge of what Mercer had done to her.

"Aaron Mercer?"

"Yeah. Mercer."

Judith set the white envelope containing the tape on the woman's desk.

"What's this?" Martha asked, picking up the envelope and sliding the tape from it.

"I want to start out by saying nobody taped that on purpose. Mercer left his telephone tape recorder on and his ... someone pulled it off the phone. Normally, I would have erased it or given it back to him, but what's on it is bothersome, Martha."

"Why don't you listen to it?"

Martha picked the tape up from her desk and turned to the credenza behind her. She carefully inserted the tape into her tape recorder.

"You might want to listen with earphones," Judith urged softly, and the woman took her advice. Thirty seconds later, she snapped off the machine. She looked up at Judith and blushed.

Judith wasn't sure what her response was going to be, but didn't expect what she heard.

"I'd prefer to forget it, Judith."

Judith sat down on one of the chairs facing Martha.

"How can you 'forget' what the man did to you in that office?"

Martha shook her head gently, her soft curls brushing the sides of her cheeks.

"It's not that I'm forgetting what he did or said, Judith. It was the most godawful embarrassing event of recent time for me. He's done it to me twice now. I know he's done it to other women in the office. I hear them talking.

It's common knowledge. But you know as well as I do that this happens everywhere. It's subtle. It's covered up in the practices of the offices. But I can live with it, because verbal's as far as it would ever go with me. For whatever reason he does this, he's never going to do anything other than be verbal with me. And I can take it, Judith, because I'm out of here in about a year. He knows that. He also knows he's the person I'm going to ask to write me a letter of recommendation. And he's the person my new employer's going to call up and chat with about me. I'm not interested in causing the man a scandal at the moment."

"Or risking the loss of a future job."

"Or risking the loss of a future job, yes."

"But I'll go to bat for you on this, Martha. I know how bad he's been to other women in this office. At some point he needs to be stopped."

It was a strange confrontation. Judith, never the active feminist, trying to persuade a colleague to publicly challenge one of the most powerful men in the office. And the colleague she was attempting to persuade was the one-time president of a women's rights organization.

"Judith, let it rest. Really, I can handle the man."

"It's not just you. What about the others he's doing this to? Don't you, we, have an obligation to keep the man from doing this again? I can *guarantee* you, if Farrell had even an inkling this was going on, he'd be through the roof and Mercer would be out of here like that." She snapped her fingers to emphasize the point. There was no way Farrell would ever tolerate any conduct that even hinted at sexual harassment.

"Oh, come on Judith, think! I go to Mercer, and what's he going to say? He's going to say there was nothing going on except having another deputy district attorney review a witness's credibility. Tough questions asked? Even embarrassing questions? Yes, of course. But that's part of the job. So who comes out the winner? Me? I don't think so. Sorry, Judith, I'm opting for job security, and I'll leave to someone else the battle of gender bias and sexual harassment in the workplace." She paused and looked at Judith. "Thanks, though, Judith. I hope you nail the bastard."

"Funny, Martha. That's the same thing Mercer's secretary told me. I'm just not sure how I'm going to be able to do that. Can I ask you a question?"

"Sure."

"Can I keep the tape?"

"Sure." Martha pressed a button and the recorder offered up the tape. She pulled it out and handed it up to Judith. "What do you plan on doing with it?"

Judith inserted the tape into the envelope.

"I'm not exactly sure. I'm not going to make you confront the man or cause any problems for you, Martha. But I'd like to keep it available, shall we say? I promise I won't do anything with it unless I talk with you first."

"Well . . . the thought doesn't exactly thrill me, but if you really need it at some point, I guess it's okay. Do me a favor, though, Judith, and not represent it as if I'm personally after the guy, you know?"

"Yeah. I know."

On the way back to her office, Judith took stock of the small but growing anti-Mercer arsenal being thrust at her. A transcript filled with embarrassing testimony read aloud by Mercer's secretary. A tape recording of Mercer asking salacious questions of a captive junior deputy. Judith had become the recipient of evidence that pointed to the man's serious character deficiency. She'd become the person a growing number of women thought could somehow help deal with the man, could maybe stop him.

Her options, though, were limited. She could go to Farrell and risk having the issue dissolve into "he said–she said," and whether or not he was asking legitimate questions of a line deputy. She could also confront Mercer directly. She'd strike a blow or two for women's rights, but perhaps that's all she would be able to accomplish, particularly since no one else seemed to be indignant enough to go to bat for herself.

She needed to wait, if for no other reason than that she needed to see what, if anything, was going to happen with her investigation into the Whaley case.

23

PIKE MARTIN RELISHED his role in the unfolding scenario. At dinner he'd had a lengthy discussion with Judith about the Whaley case. He'd looked at the man's files and noted the same consistencies with the Russell case that Judith herself had noted. There was no doubt in his mind that if he were prosecuting Whaley, he'd have included the attack on Caryn Russell as one of the offenses. He understood the imperative nature of his task now. He was charged not only with seeing what ties existed between Whaley and the Russell girl's attack, but with doing so before the preliminary hearing.

He was fortunate. Whaley hadn't been sent up to the state prison system yet. He was still in San Diego's county jail, awaiting transportation. He'd pleaded guilty "straight up" to the face of the complaint on two of his victims, and with his history of four prior felony convictions, he was, under California's three-strikes law, on his way to state prison for a minimum of sixty years, which amounted to a life term for him.

With such a severe sentence facing Whaley, the man would be in a position to be candid about whether he was the perpetrator of the attack on Caryn Russell. On the other hand, with his extensive criminal background, Whaley had nothing to lose by denying involvement and telling Pike to take a hike. He had nothing to gain in the sentencing department. The prosecutor who took the plea wouldn't be giving Whaley any leeway for admitting he had another child victim tucked away in his recent past.

Pike waited for the doors of the holding tank to roll open. The familiar sound of metal grinding against metal meant Whaley was being ushered into the room.

The guard bringing Whaley in walked him to the table where Pike was seated. Whaley wasn't handcuffed. Pike would have asked for restraints if he'd felt they were needed.

"Shall I stay?" the guard asked.

"Unnecessary," Pike responded. "Mr. Whaley and I won't be long."

The guard turned to leave. "I'll be outside the door, then."

Pike took a few moments to orient himself to Whaley. The man's appearance hadn't changed since his booking photo. His cheeks were pockmarked from acne. His face was long, his chin protruding slightly. The eyes were a little more sunken, his skin more sallow. But those were attributable to his stay in jail.

The first matter of business was to Mirandize the man. Pike had brought along his portable tape recorder to substantiate his advisement of rights. He knew he was subject to complaints for having spoken to the man without his attorney being present. But the law was sufficiently ambiguous to allow Pike some leeway. What he wanted was information only. The chances of Whaley being charged with another offense were not high. What Pike wanted was an admission of any kind. And he was prepared to do some bargaining for the admission. His mission was not to hang Whaley; it was to release Russell. He was prepared to be up front about his mission.

"Mr. Whaley, my name's Pike Martin. I'm an investigator with the police department. I'm familiar with your past offenses and the status of your current cases and your current sentence. Mind if I turn my recorder on, Mr. Whaley? Just to protect the both of us?"

"Go ahead. But I'd like to know what this is about."

"Well, you don't have to talk to me at all, Mr. Whaley. I'm here to talk to you. You don't have to say anything."

Whaley eyed Pike cautiously.

"Shoot."

Pike pushed the record button on his machine.

"Testing—one, two, three." He played it back to verify it was recording, then started it again, recording his name, location, date, and time. Then he read the *Miranda* rights to Whaley, informing him, among other things, that he had a right to have an attorney present during the taping. He held his breath while Whaley paused briefly and indicated he was willing to listen to what Pike had to say without having an attorney present. Pike then got directly to the point of his visit.

"There's another little girl who was attacked in the general area you admitted kidnapping and attacking the other girls. There's another man accused of attacking that other girl. Her name's Caryn. Here's her picture." Pike removed a three-by-five-inch school photo of the girl and placed it before Whaley, who picked it up briefly, glanced at it, and put it down again. "This is a picture of her house. I'm not giving you address. It's close to the other victims' homes." Pike took a photo of the Russell home from his file and laid it before Whaley. Again the man picked it up, looked at it, and handed it back to Pike.

"This is the man who's charged with the crime." They followed the same procedure. "He's tried to kill himself. His marriage is falling apart. The girl says her father didn't do it, but there's a lot of pressure on her to say he did. She's about to be called to testify at the preliminary hearing against her father. You know what that means, right? Her father pleads guilty to keep her off the stand, and if he doesn't and she testifies, the prosecutor yanks the plea. No plea. It goes to a jury. Even if he's found not guilty, the damage is done."

"Well. . . ."

"Don't say anything, Mr. Whaley. That was the deal. I want you to think about what I just told you. Talk to your attorney and get back to me. Here's my card."

Pike reached into the pocket of his jacket, took a small white card from it, and placed it in front of Whaley. Have your attorney call me."

"What if I don't have an attorney?"

"Call me. If you want to talk, we'll get you one, okay?"

"Fair enough. If I want to talk."

"At this point, you don't have anything to lose. You're heading to prison for a long time. If this guy didn't do it, he's got a lot more to lose."

"What do I get out of this?"

Pike smirked. "A warm fuzzy feeling."

Whaley grinned back. "Not enough."

"I'm not in a position to hand out bargains. That's up to your attorney and the prosecutor."

"Then I'll think about it, Mr. Martin."

"Okay. I'm turning off the recorder now."

Pike snapped the recorder off, stood, and walked to the door. He knocked once and it opened, the guard outside stepping into the room and standing over Whaley, who remained seated. As the guard stood by, Whaley rose and faced Pike.

"There is something I'd like, Mr. Martin. . . ."

As much as Pike wanted to jump on the request, the presence of the guard and the lack of defense counsel caused him to say only, "Call me, Mr. Whaley. Think about it and call me."

"I will. Maybe sooner than you think."

As Whaley was led out of the room, Pike gathered up his files and tape recorder. The fish was on the hook. Now he needed a defense counsel who could help him reel Whaley in.

24

PIKE WAS MIDWAY through his foil-wrapped lunch, a fast-food selection of greasy tacos and overcooked beef enchiladas. Outside, storm clouds were gathering, and the pace of business at the office seemed to slow down in anticipation of a downpour. The morning had been relatively quiet. No homicides reported. One armed robbery of a convenience store. Two domestic disputes. When the phone rang, Pike didn't recognize the voice at the other end. It took several minutes to orient himself to the caller's request. It was Whaley. He wanted to talk.

Pike was cautious.

"Mr. Whaley, I'm glad you've decided to talk about the Russell case, but I want to say right off that I can't do that because you don't have an attorney and you need to talk to one when we get together again."

"I didn't say I wanted to talk about the Russell case exactly, Mr. Martin."

"Then what did you call me for, ain't no way it was to brighten my morning."

229

Pike could hear Whaley chuckle. "No, I'm not shootin' to brighten up your day, here, Detective. It's that I'm only goin' to be at the jail a few more days before they ship me out. I just wanna, you know. . . ."

"No, I don't know. Why don't you tell me? But hurry. My lunch's getting cold."

It was a cat-and-mouse game, and they both knew it. Pike couldn't be too overanxious to talk to the man. There was no telling what he was calling for, if he wanted to cut a deal or just see what might be dangled in front of him in return for his cooperation. Whaley wanted to talk, but not until he could cut some kind of deal for something in return for his cooperation. What that might be was open for discussion. His sentence was set. He wasn't going to get anything more than he'd already been given, which wasn't much. So this conversation was the opening.

"I just wanna talk."

"You need an attorney first. You got one?"

"No. Not now, My trial attorney had me sign a Notice of Appeal for my case, but I guess that's the last I seen of him."

"You know one you want to call?"

"Not really."

"I can't talk about it over the phone, you know that."

"Tell me when and where."

"You want us to contact the court and get you an appointed attorney?"

"Yeah. And they'll contact me?"

"Whoever it is will contact you."

Pike scraped the last forkful of enchilada

from the foil tray and shoveled it into his mouth, barely swallowing before dialing the phone.

As she reviewed the cases on her desk, Judith paused every so often to watch the rain falling outside an office window coated with months of accumulated dirt. Thoughts of her mother intruded. It happened that way. They popped up at unexpected times and without any attempt by Judith to cause them. She'd be driving down the street after a busy day or driving from dropping Elizabeth off somewhere and a song would come on the radio that reminded her of something her mother had done or said, and that would be enough to start tears. Sometimes there was nothing in particular, like this rain. And sometimes her thoughts were purely of the physical, and at times, they seemed strange and even bizarre avenues. What did her mother look like now? It was not an entirely benign train of thought. It seeped into her life in odd, inexplicable ways. She could look at someone and tell what they would look like when they were dead. This phenomenon she attributed to her watching a normal face and body, an active mind, die over a long period of time. You can't experience that without it changing your view of life itself, she knew that. Judith sighed, reassuring herself. She was still too close to the death. It would take time.

The telephone's ringing was a welcome sound, and the deep, raspy voice yelling at her on the opposite end, launching into a conversation almost in midthought, made her smile.

"The son of a bitch wants to talk, can you believe that?"

"Which son of a bitch wants to talk, Pike?"

"Whaley."

She sat forward at her desk. "The Whaley, as in Russell?"

"The very same one."

"How do you know that?"

"He just called me."

Judith's heart skipped a beat. Pike was notorious for launching into probes without thinking through the necessary procedures. She was constantly reigning him in.

"Pike, you didn't. . . ."

"Don't worry. I haven't done anything wrong. He wants to talk, and I told him he needed to talk to an attorney first. The problem is, he doesn't have an attorney now."

"You didn't promise him anything. . . ."

"Nothing. He wants something, though. That's clear. I didn't ask . . . I just told him he needs an attorney. He had his own attorney representing him up through sentencing. But he might need to talk to someone on the appointed lists for this."

"I can take care of that, Pike. I'll give the public defender's office a call. This is pretty sensitive. We want him to talk about Caryn Russell, about a case he could be charged in if he did it. He doesn't have to say a thing. He's already spending about the rest of his life in prison." Her voice inflection rose slightly. "Maybe we can appeal to his sense of justice."

There was a sputtering noise at the other

end of the phone. Judith could picture Pike, coffee mug in hand, trying to swallow her last comment.

"I'll give you a call later, Pike, and let you know what's happening."

Judith glanced up. It was 11 o'clock. The director of the public defender's office would be in. Her hand reached for the Rolodex next to the phone and less than a minute later the director, Chuck Ramert, answered.

Chuck was barely an acquaintance of Judith's. He was a tall, thin man who wore the pale, gaunt look of the long-distance runner he was. Like her, he was almost exclusively an administrator, hence their paths seldom crossed.

"I have a guy on his way to state prison, Chuck, for assaults against several children. We may be charging him with another related sex offense against a different minor. He wants to talk but needs a lawyer."

"Where are you in the charging stage, Judith, or are you not interested in an additional prison sentence?" There was a hint of sarcasm in his voice. Prosecutors were usually interested in prison time regardless of the number of offenses.

"Well, I can't guarantee anything at this point. What concerns me is that there's another guy in jail facing his preliminary hearing on that same offense. If Whaley did it, and I have to tell you it's very similar, Chuck, then an innocent guy's about to take a dive for him."

"Well, if you guys over there would stop

filing death penalty cases at the drop of a hat
and use a little discretion, I wouldn't have any
trouble finding someone for you. But I've got
three attorneys tied up full time on death penalty cases, so they're out. Everyone else's
booked solid. What's your time frame on
Whaley?"

"Pretty quick. We don't have a charging
document yet, but it's on the way. You get
someone in there to talk to him and I'll enter-
tain a plea. How generous a plea, I don't
know. It depends on whether his story holds
together. Have the attorney come by and take
a look at our files. That'll be faster than tracking down the private attorney who represented him."

"I'm looking at my list of available attorneys
right now, Judith." He began mumbling under
his breath, Judith catching only fragments of
names. "I've got Jess Allen, Paul Kline, Alan
Larson, Michael Addison. . . ."

Judith let him finish reciting the list of available attorneys.

*She didn't dare! Yet, the temptation! The sce-
nario laid itself out before her. Larson has Russell.
If he got Whaley, he'd make the connection. And
in the hands of a capable attorney like Larson, Russell might get the ammunition he needed. Still, if
she hinted she liked Larson, Chuck Ramert would
surely give her someone else.*

"I'm in no position to interfere, obviously,
but Mike Addison's as good as it gets in these
sensitive child molests. If he's free, he'd be
great, and I might just take this one on myself." She bit her lip. "Alan Larson and I just

don't seem to have had a good rapport in the past."

There was a slight pause on the other end of the phone. She could just see Chuck Ramert's eyes bulging and his upper lip curl into the slight snarl that characterized his more contentious moments in court. She knew what he was thinking: *How dare this woman presume to tell me who to appoint to a case?*

Judith closed her eyes and crossed the fingers of her right hand. He wouldn't appoint Addison now for all the money in the world. But would he appoint Larson?

"No, Mike's really got a full plate. I'm thinking maybe Alan Larson. He's just had a capital death case shut down on him.

Judith's heart skipped. *Yes!*

But the elation was short lived as she struggled with her conscience. She was sure Larson was not set up to make the connection. But in truth, she and Larson were bitter adversaries. Judith and he had tangled in court more than once, and on each occasion it had been a wholly unsatisfactory experience. He was an arrogant, self-centered, win-oriented attorney who'd stop at nothing for the sake of his client. Despite his great reviews and his immense trial talent, as far as she was concerned, he skirted the edge of propriety in the courtroom. Now she was about to do the same, for the thought of handing him Whaley's file, to compare outright with the files of Russell, a defendant being handled by a colleague in her office, was just beyond questionable. She closed her eyes. For all Larson's faults, he was exactly the attorney Russell needed.

"I'll send a memo over to Alan and ask him to take it. He'll be giving you a call."

Judith opened her eyes and said, "I'll be ready."

25

IT TOOK LESS than forty-eight hours for Larson to call on Judith, but she'd been expecting a visit far sooner. He checked in at the main reception desk and had the secretary there call her. She was ready for him. The Whaley files were sitting on her desk, and she'd even placed paper clips at the pages she wanted to draw attention to. How long, she wondered, would it take for him to catch on?

"Alan! Come in. It's good to see you." She stood and extended her hand. "Have a seat and I'll explain what we've got. I guess I should ask you first if you've had a chance to talk with Whaley."

He took one of the chairs opposite her desk and instead of going back to her desk to sit, Judith took the second chair, seating herself right next to him. She pulled the interior tray from the desk front. It was a seating arrangement she usually reserved for colleagues coming into her office to discuss cases. It was far friendlier than over-the-desk discussions.

"No, I haven't. Not yet, anyway. I thought

I'd come take a look at the files, then have a talk with him. It'll give me a better understanding of what I'm dealing with."

Judith had every intention of being accommodating and he was making it easy. No hardball. She reached across the desk and pulled the Whaley files toward her.

"You can take these to the library, if you want, and you can photocopy whatever you need. But let me summarize them for you. Whaley's accused of raping and/or molesting these victims. You'll see the ages, they're all less than nine years old. It's a bizarre combination of motive and opportunity. He enters their houses at night while they're sleeping, through bedroom windows." She could see Larson's eyes widen.

"He actually carries them outside, takes them on walks or drives them around, molests them, then drives them home. There's the threat, 'Don't tell, or I'll kill you and your family.' And all the girls are about a mile or two from each other on the east side of town."

Larson began massaging his chin with his right hand. He was getting nervous. Judith continued.

"I know the factual scenarios are bizarre. At first no one believed the girls, but apparently Whaley assaulted the daughter of one of his buddies and his conscience got the best of him. He confessed to the dad, who beat him up and called the police. We wouldn't take anything other than a plea straight up to the face of the complaints. He's looking at the rest of his life in prison. Then there's this other case, against a man named Thomas Russell. He's accused of molesting a little girl, his own daughter, I think." She paused. "You want some coffee, Alan?"

His answer was barely a whisper. "No, no thanks."

She feigned a lapse in memory. "Yeah, where was I?"

"Russell . . . Thomas Russell."

"Right. Well, his daughter says he didn't do it. She's persistent about it, but who knows, by the time the preliminary hearing rolls around, she'll say whatever the prosecutor wants her to say, right?"

Larson didn't answer. His mind was racing. She could see it. He thought he'd made a startling discovery no one else knew about. *Fool prosecutor,* he must be thinking. She smiled. It was amusing, watching him fidget now, casting fleeting glances toward the Whaley files on her desk. He couldn't wait.

"It might be interesting looking at the locations of all three crimes, Alan. They're very close."

Suddenly Larson stopped fidgeting. The hand resting near the Whaley files withdrew and the look of hunger on his face gave way to sudden calm. His chin dropped and his brow knitted. He stared at Judith so intensely as to cause her to pull back in her chair.

"Something wrong, Alan?"

"Do you know what you're doing? What kind of trouble you're asking for?"

He knew. He knew exactly what she was doing. How fast he'd figured it out!

Judith leaned forward, unwilling to acknowledge his discovery.

"I intend to charge Whaley with the crimes against Caryn Russell. That's all I have to say right now."

"You know I represent. . . ."

She didn't let him finish.

"I said I fully intend to prosecute the man."

"Wait a minute, what's. . . ."

Judith reached over, picked up the Whaley files, and placed them on the tray between them.

"Alan, I think you need to look at these. Give them back to the receptionist, will you, when you're done?"

He knew what she was doing, but he didn't know why. And that was going to drive the man crazy. His voice was steady and direct.

"I don't like this, Judith. Even *I* don't like this."

Judith stood, picked up the files, and extended them to Larson.

"Alan," she said softly, "it seems to me you're going to have a field day."

Larson stood and took the files from her, content for the moment to accept what was unfolding before him.

"Sure. I get to sail one client down the river to save another client. Isn't that some kind of ethical problem?"

He was right. There was a huge ethical problem defending one client on the grounds that another had committed the crime. Maybe he could keep both clients. And then again, maybe he'd have to choose which one he wanted to continue representing, make a decision which one was telling the truth. But it was only fitting that if she was going to hand Larson a plum, he was going to have to struggle to hold onto it—

"You're not going to have to get to the point where you have to make a choice between clients, Alan. Just start with Whaley, will you? Because I *am* going to charge Mr. Whaley with assaulting Caryn Russell."

"And you, Judith, how about you?"

"Me?"

"You know who the prosecutor is on the Russell case?"

"Aaron Mercer's the prosecutor."

"You folks over here always cut each other's throats like this?"

"No. I have reasons . . . and I'll just have to take my chances."

For the first time since their meeting had begun, Judith smiled, having made a connection with a distant moment somewhere out on a green field in the middle of the afternoon.

"Who knows, Alan, maybe the referee won't see me."

""Like hell the referee won't. The only thing I can tell you, Judith, is that I have to do whatever I have to do to protect my clients. I'm not going to push you on why you're doing this. I assume you have some pretty good reasons. And I hope at some point you're going to let me know what they are."

Judith smiled again. "I'm sure I will."

"I'll get the files back this afternoon. I guess

I should be saying thanks, but I'm not sure yet for what."

"Like I said, you can use the photocopier in the library."

She waited until he walked out the door before returning to her chair behind the desk. Larson was right. She'd handed him up one terrific set of arguments. He could defend Russell on the grounds that some other dude did it, that dude being Whaley. Or he could defend Whaley on the grounds that Russell did it. He might have to give one of them up as a client. On the other hand, he just might pull off a plea bargain for Whaley and a walk out the door for Russell. As for her, she'd already done what she'd set out to do, which was to give Russell a fighting chance.

Unfortunately, Mercer wasn't going to see it the same way.

26

THE CLERK STARED at the signature, then looked up at the man who'd requested to check out the files. She recognized Alan Larson, so no personal identification was necessary. "I'll be right back, Mr. Larson. Were you going to check the files out, or look at them here at the counter?"

"I'll be checking them out for the afternoon."

"You know you can't take them out of the library."

Alan Larson smiled. Some attorneys were allowed to take the files from the file room to the counsel library on the third floor. Larson was not. Given his reputation for trial shenanigans, the word was out that he was to be kept on a short leash by all district attorney personnel.

"I know. I plan on being here for a while."

The clerk disappeared behind a door and several minutes later emerged with a file log. She wrote the names and case numbers in a black log book and passed the files back to

Larson, who took them to a small desk at the corner of the file room. The only chair available was a large heavy wooden one with no seat pad, and he had to pull that one from the opposite end of the room. It was not the best of conditions for a man who liked to spread out his work.

One by one, Larson opened each file to generally orient himself to the offenses. He liked to start with the probation reports prepared for sentencing. They were usually complete chronological accounts of the case and any related offenses, along with all background reports, including psychologicals on the defendant.

The desk was barely large enough for Larson's own pad of white lined paper and one file. The remaining files he placed on the floor next to him.

Larson combed the files, scribbling copious, seemingly unorganized notes. He was looking for patterns, repetitive conduct, and similarities in the victims or the manner in which the crimes were committed. After an hour, the similarities between the Russell girl's attack and assaults on Whaley's victims were overwhelming. After an hour more, Larson was convinced the crimes might be related and he fully intended to file a motion in the Russell case asking the judge to allow him to introduce evidence that another person—Whaley—might have committed the crime. There were several obstacles to his plan, though. The biggest was Aaron Mercer. He could ask Mercer to look at the information on Whaley and perhaps appeal to Mercer's sense of justice. He had his doubts Mercer would allow it, but it was the required first step, and it would be done in a formal way, through a motion Larson would file with the judge who would preside at the preliminary hearing.

Even before the motion, however, Larson needed to talk with Whaley.

Alan Larson sat at the counsel table in the small interview room adjoining the jail holding tank, listening for the heavy metallic clank of the jail doors that signaled Arthur Whaley was on his way in to talk with him. He'd not yet met his newest client or even talked with him on the phone. Because his role was hopefully going to be limited to accommodating a beneficial plea bargain for the man, he intended to take each step slowly. His first step would be to establish whether Whaley had committed the attack on Caryn Russell.

He didn't like asking his clients if they'd committed the crimes with which they were charged. It was his philosophy that every defendant required a fair trial and his job was to be sure they got it, whether they were innocent or guilty, no matter how reprehensible the crimes involved. Knowing whether they were actually guilty introduced mental elements into the representation that only clouded his judgment.

The Whaley case would be an exception. He had to satisfy himself that Whaley was guilty in order to satisfy himself that he could represent both Whaley and Russell. It had to be a fair tradeoff between the men, and Larson intended to be up front about his plan.

At last the familiar sounds roused Larson from his chair. The door to the interview room opened and Arthur Whaley stepped inside, a deputy sheriff walking directly behind the man. Larson was glad to see Whaley wasn't handcuffed. His hands were instead tucked into the front waistband of his jail uniform.

"Arthur Whaley?"

Whaley nodded but didn't remove his hands to offer a handshake.

Larson dismissed the guard and asked Whaley to sit down.

"I'm Alan Larson from the public defender's office."

"Yeah. The detective tol' me someone would come over to see me about some case or somethin' about a little girl."

"What detective?"

"Ah, a guy named Martin."

"Martin? Pike Martin?"

"Uh-huh. He jus' tol' me there was another case, and if I wanted an attorney, he'd see that I got one. I guess you's him, am I right?"

"Yeah. I'm him. This detective, did you say anything to him about the case he's interested in? A case about a girl named Caryn Russell?"

"Nah. He didn't want to talk 'til I saw a lawyer. I tol' him I wanted an attorney and he stopped taping."

"He taped your conversation?"

"Yeah. He taped it to be sure no one said he was a bad detective, you know."

"Did he give you the *Miranda* rights? Do you know what those are?"

"Do I know the *Miranda* rights? Of course I do. He read 'em off a little card."

"Arthur, I need to talk to you about a couple of things, and I want to make them really clear, so if you have any questions, you'll let me know?"

"Go ahead, I'm with you so far."

"The first thing I'll need to tell you is that I'm representing the man accused of attacking Caryn Russell."

A puzzled look spread over Whaley's face. "Wait a minute, wait a minute. I ain't no lawyer, but there's a problem, right? How you gonna go to court for him and me?"

"I really can't. It's called an ethical conflict. I can represent the both of you if it works to both your advantage and you know what's happening and why and agree to it."

"So? What's in this for me?"

"At this point the district attorney's going to charge you with the attack on the Caryn Russell girl."

"And the other guy, too?"

"Uh-huh."

"That's crazy."

"It is. But there doesn't seem to be a whole lot I can do about it."

"I'm going away for a long time on three cases already. What's one more going to do to me?"

"Are you asking me or telling me?"

"I'm just making a comment. But what *is* it going to do to me?"

"If you're lucky, not a lot. You work out a plea bargain that doesn't affect you too much. Maybe concurrent time for the other because it happened before your convictions on the other three cases. That is, if you're guilty."

Whaley leaned back in his chair.

"Okay, and how do I go about doing that?"

"Your lawyer would do that for you. That's up to him to do."

"You can do that?"

"I'd be hopeful. I've done it before."

"Well, let's see if they file a case on me, and if they do, I'll let you see if you can get me some concurrent time on this new case. And one other thing I want. . . ."

Larson waved his hand in the air. "Just a minute. Slow down here. I wouldn't do anything unless I was satisfied you were guilty."

"I was convicted of three attacks. I committed five in San Diego. Wanna hear about them?"

"No! No, just one, against a girl named Caryn Russell. She lived very near the other three."

"What's she look like?"

"Blond, curls. About six years old. Thin."

Whaley continued Larson's description. "White house. Blue shutters on the window. Bedroom window on the first floor."

"Close enough. She described an assailant who looks a lot like you, Arthur."

"I s'pose there's a reason for that."

"Maybe. But she's given a crazy story about being taken out of her house, then assaulted and having the guy buy her ice cream."

Whaley's mouth stretched into a wide grin. "Hey, what's so strange about that?"

"At two A.M.?"

"It happens."

"What ice cream store's open 'til 2 A.M.?"

"Ah, drugstores are open that long."

"She says the guy had a black car with a license plate that had mountains on it."

"Like from Colorado?"

Larson didn't reply. Whaley continued for him.

"Who's the guy charged with her attack?"

"Her father."

Whaley puckered his lips and whistled.

"That's got to be hard on the ol' family thing."

"Yeah, it's hard on the family thing. The father, Tom Russell, he's in jail."

"And the kid?"

"She's at home. For now."

"Any chance you can clear him without finding the real attacker?"

"I don't think so."

"Well, I might be interested in a bargain, you know?"

"Yeah, I know. What kind of bargain you can get is up in the air."

"Well, I have some ideas of what I want."

"We'll talk about that if it becomes necessary. I need to ask you if you have any problems with me representing you and Russell."

"If I plead guilty, what difference does it make?"

Larson stood to leave. "I guess you're right,

but I'd feel better if I can get your agreement in writing."

"I'll do that." Whaley raised one finger in the air. "If you can get me concurrent time in prison." He raised a second finger. "And my books."

27

WHEN JUDITH ARRIVED at Mercer's office, the door was closed. Nobody entered when his door was closed.

"What's up with Aaron today?" Judith asked his secretary. "Is he alone in there?"

"Oh, yeah, he's alone, all right. And not very happy. Something's given him a fit."

Judith was waiting for the shoe to drop and this might be it. It was only a matter of time before Mercer found out Judith was charging Whaley with the same offenses he'd charged against Russell. When he did, he'd be angry and brood for a while about it. Then there'd undoubtedly be a visit to Farrell's office. Judith hadn't yet prepared herself for that eventuality, but this was obviously the time to begin thinking about it.

As Judith turned toward her office, Mercer's office door flew open and he emerged. He spotted her immediately.

"Judith!" he yelled.

He must be angry, she thought. *He didn't call me "Jude."*

"Judith! I need to talk with you right away. Can you come in?"

She didn't respond, but headed toward him. As she did, he retreated into his office, waiting for her just inside the door, closing it behind her as she entered.

"Judith, I can't believe what I found out this morning. I got this call from Alan Larson. I wasn't in, but he left a message on my tape recorder that he was representing Arthur Whaley on charges he committed the crimes against Caryn Russell! That's impossible because I've charged the girl's father with that crime, you know that! I haven't been able to talk with the man, but how can that be? We don't have two cases with two different defendants for the same crime."

He didn't know her involvement yet. She could tell him she'd check on it and wait for a better moment. But there wasn't going to be any better moment.

"Aaron?"

He was at his desk staring at the phone, drumming his fingers noisily on the gleaming wood.

"Aaron, I'm bringing the charges against Whaley." She wanted to be strong and honest about her involvement, but her voice was a whisper.

"Aaron, I don't think you heard me, maybe?"

"You what, Judith?"

"I'm filing charges against Whaley."

"I'm sorry, Judith, *what* charges are you filing against Whaley?"

"The assault against Caryn."

"Russell?"

"Yes. I, I intended to tell you—"

"No, no, now just a second, here. Are you telling me that you're actually going to file charges against a defendant knowing I'm prosecuting someone for the same offenses?"

Judith could feel her knees weakening. "I think Russell's innocent. Take a look at the Whaley files and you'll see the crimes are almost identical to the Russell assault."

Mercer, not ready to respond directly to Judith, mumbled to himself. "There's a deep, deep violation of office protocol here. A deep violation."

He rose and walked toward Judith, stopping squarely before her, his disbelief turning to anger.

"Judith, I know we haven't exactly seen eye to eye on the Russell case. You think one way on it and I think another way. But you have no right to interfere with my case, no right whatsoever. The only question is what you're going to do about it, because I have no intention of dropping the charges against Russell. Larson'll try to bring in the crimes you've charged, but I'm telling you right now, if you want a battle over this, you're going to get it. This is about the most infuriating, underhanded tactic I've ever seen."

Judith wanted to say something, but she couldn't. She had no defense to offer, because despite her beliefs, Mercer was right. She could only watch as Mercer pushed past her into the hallway, headed in the direction of Farrell's office.

Judith stood for a moment staring out Mercer's door, listening to the silence. The office staff could hear everything Mercer said as he stormed away. She waited uneasily a few minutes more, then exited, trying hard to maintain her composure by not making eye contact with the secretarial staff. Any emotional letdown now would be a major concession to Mercer. Only out of the corner of her eye did she see Mercer's secretary staring in her direction, the thumb of her right hand extended upward, a sign of victory.

Some victory.

Victory meant Farrell's agreement that she'd acted properly, and that was not going to happen.

For the first time in their relationship, Judith felt uncomfortable facing Lawrence Farrell. The discomfort was in large part due to the length of time it took Farrell to call her. She'd expected he would want to see her immediately after her encounter with Mercer. But he'd waited. And she knew why. He was angry.

"Have a seat, Judith."

He watched in silence as she sank to the edge of one of the chairs opposite his desk.

"You know why I need to talk with you."

"I can guess."

"Well, I've been sitting here trying to figure out what could possibly be motivating you. Your conduct's inexplicable. Do you have a reason for charging a man with a crime when

another deputy in this office is charging someone else with it? And while you're thinking
about an answer, you might want to add some
reason why you didn't tell the other deputy
what you were doing. Or perhaps even let me
in on it?"

"Thomas Russell's not guilty of the crime.
Whaley is."

"And what's that conclusion based on?"

"Evidence."

"Like what evidence, Judith?"

"It's being developed."

His right eyebrow raised noticeably.

"Developed by whom? And if you say it's
defense counsel, I'll—"

She didn't want him to finish the sentence.
"Just give me a little time."

Farrell shook his head. "Can't do that, Judith. Can't have two cases proceeding like this.
It's Aaron's case. It's Aaron's call. I'm instruct-
ing you to drop the charges against Whaley."

"If you're worried about how this looks in
your election . . ."

"My election has nothing to do with this,
Judith, and you know better than that. It has
to do with the way an office is run. You're
wrong on this one. If you don't drop the
charges, I will."

"You're going to have to do that, then,
Larry. I can't drop the charges against a man
who's guilty."

Farrell shrugged. "If that's what needs to be
done."

A wave of nausea swept over her. She was
angry as well, but not at anyone or anything

in particular. She was doing the wrong thing for the right reason, and unless Farrell was willing to let her have some rope on this one, the game was over. From the looks of things, Farrell wasn't budging. Judith nodded and took two steps backward before turning and walking from the office. She glanced at her watch. It was 4:45. At the elevator she hesitated and pressed the down button, electing not to return to her office and perhaps risk having to confront Mercer.

28

JUDITH SAT AT the glass table in the break-fast area watching Elizabeth kick the soccer ball against the concrete wall separating their yard from the neighbor. To the west the sun was setting, and the sky was ablaze in orange and red. No one had called her after she'd left the office. She was certain that by midmorning the following day the charges against Whaley would be dismissed, and with the dismissal, Larson's ethical problems would disappear and hers would just be starting. Whatever those problems might be, however, she was willing to leave to others. At the moment, she was absorbed in Elizabeth's kicking, long, hard hits she'd not seen before. She usually dropped Elizabeth at the field or used the car-pool of parents and children who lived in the area and commuted north after school.

Judith watched until Elizabeth stopped and approached.

"Ready for dinner, Liz?"

"No! Don't even mention food. Not yet. All I want is something to drink." With this declaration she dribbled the soccer ball into the house and disappeared with it down the hallway.

"Yell when you're hungry!"

Judith sat until the sky settled into a darkening sky before returning to the house. She walked down the hallway toward Elizabeth's room, and, finding she was in the shower, walked the long hallway back toward the kitchen. She wanted to wait until Elizabeth could tell her what she might want for dinner. Until then, she had nothing to do.

Judith wandered toward her mother's bedroom and looked in. She came down to this end of the house so infrequently now. Nothing much had changed. The same bedspread covered the bed. The same curtains. . . .

Judith rolled the closet door open. Her mother's clothes, mostly brightly colored housecoats, were smashed up against each other. Judith removed one of them, a light blue cotton. Taking it from the hanger, she folded it halfwise by length then in half again, making a neat square of it. She let it fall to the floor and took another from the closet and let it, too, drop to the floor, this time without the dignity of the square folds. One by one she emptied the closet. Every once in a while, some dress would make her stop, and because it aroused memories too dear to toss away, she would hang it back in the closet. Periodically, she sneezed, as examination of an item, particularly those at the back of the closet, loosened months, and in some cases years, of dust.

Judith hadn't been planning to empty the

closet of her mother's belongings that night. Indeed, she hadn't even offered a thought in that direction. But standing alone in the kitchen, she'd made an instantaneous decision to do something physical, and the closet in the bedroom was there, ready to be rearranged.

It was time. Time to clear away some of the past. She felt it come on so fast she hadn't thought about it. Then it became just a function.

While the pace at the outset was halting, it quickened as she fell into a pattern, and by the time Elizabeth appeared in the doorway asking what was for dinner, clothing littered the bedroom floor. There were two basic piles, one for Goodwill, one for the Women's Shelter. In the middle, clothing and shoes too old or in too poor a condition to give away were strewn loosely about.

Within fifteen minutes the clothes were stuffed into three white plastic garbage bags with black ink scrawled across each of them indicating who they would be delivered to.

When she was done, Judith stood back and looked at the clothes now hung neatly in the closet. There weren't many items of clothing, but those that she kept meant something special to her; a present she'd bought for her mother, a shopping trip, the dresses she wore when she'd been dressed up by Jean to sit outside. She'd never throw them away. How strange it seemed to her that those dresses would probably be there in the closet until she died or moved from the house.

In the kitchen, Judith found Elizabeth rummaging through the cupboards in search of something to snack on. Too exhausted to begin a full dinner, she let the girl continue foraging and made soup and sandwiches.

When the last of the dinner dishes were washed and Elizabeth was in bed, Judith finally sat at the television set, within minutes dozing off, awakening at the sound of the electronic music announcing the 11 P.M. news. She checked the doors to see if they were locked and turned off the lights as she made her way down the hallway to her bedroom. In the back of her mind was the vague thought that she'd have to deal with Mercer in the morning.

29

JUDITH WAS IN her office earlier than usual, for no reason other than wanting to be there before Mercer arrived. Perhaps it was a psychological advantage she hoped to gain, but in the end to no avail. Mercer was there before she was, smiling and nodding in her direction, then heading for his office. It was just like him to say nothing, at least until he felt it was to his advantage.

At 8:30 the telephone buzzer sounded. It was Alan Larson.

"I told you you'd never get away with it, Judith. You know the complaint against Whaley's been dismissed?"

"I know. I was informed in no uncertain terms last night."

"It was dismissed at five o'clock yesterday."

"They're making a mistake and they don't seem to care, Alan."

Unexpectedly, he laughed. "I've been trying to tell you folks for years. You make mistakes all the time."

"Yeah, sure we do. This is the only one I

261

can remember in a while." She paused a moment. "At the risk of again betraying the trust of everyone around here, I assume you read the files and realize Whaley's crimes are not only similar to the Russell incident, but geographically very close to the Russell girl's house."

"Well, at the risk of violating my own sacred trust to my client—that's Whalley I'm talking about—I know all that. And more. Russell's not your man. He's just not. And he'd have been out of jail a long time ago if his first attorney had bothered to go out to the Russell house and look around. And where's the lab evidence? Why no DNA tests? What about the footprints on the windowsill and the park where she was molested being close by? Why not check out her story to see if the all-night drugstore sold ice cream? What in the name of God do you folks do there?" He wanted to tell her Whaley had all but admitted his guilt, but he couldn't bring himself to do that. There was no need at this point. He knew Whalley was guilty. Judith did, too. Other than that, Larson's tirade was mostly for effect. He knew this case was an aberration.

"They're not all like this, Alan. You know they're not. The question is, what's going to happen to Russell now?"

"He's headed for a preliminary hearing three days from now. His daughter's going to be called to testify against him. I'm going to object on the grounds I don't have the labwork back and I don't have the kind of criminal discovery I need for trial, but the judge is going to deny my request to continue the hearing. He's also going to deny my request to introduce evidence someone else committed the offenses. Russell will probably be bound over for trial, and I'll have to make as much trouble as I can in Superior Court. Of course, when he's bound over for trial, our friend Mercer's not going to talk plea bargain. So, my client's dead in the water."

"There's got to be a way out."

"Not with Mercer, there's not."

"Alan . . . did you hear the interview Pike had with Whaley?"

"No, not that I recall. It's not with the evidence, is it?"

"Pike may still have it."

"Is it something I ought to listen to?"

"Might not be a bad idea to introduce it. See what you think . . . I'm sorry, I can't talk to you this way anymore, I mean, telling you what to introduce."

"I never listen to prosecution advice, Judith. You know that."

"You said that already . . ."

"But I will this time. Anything interesting on it?"

"Something like admissions by Whaley."

"They'll never come in. Mercer'll never let it in."

"He doesn't have to, just let the judge hear it in order to rule on it. Promise? With Mercer there, too. Okay? And I need to talk with you before that hearing."

"Oh, God, I'm making a promise to a prosecutor. You can't see me, but I'm holding my nose. I . . . I promise! There. That satisfy you?"

"I'm not sure yet. But it has some real possibility. Some very real possibilities."

There was a slight knock on the office door. It was Mercer, motioning he'd come back when she was off the phone. She waved him into the office.

"Gotta go. Aaron's here. I'll call you later."

"Say hi to him for me, will you, Judith?"

"Sure I will. I'll be certain to do that. Better yet, you want to do that right now?"

"Actually, no, thanks. I'll talk to you later." He hung up without waiting for her reply.

Judith replaced the receiver on the cradle.

"What can I do for you, Aaron?"

He took several steps backward and turned, reaching for the door handle. "Mind if I close the door?" He hadn't intended anything other than closing it. Her response was irrelevant.

There was a feeling of discomfort, a vague feeling of danger. She minded. She minded a lot. But she didn't tell him. Had she been honest with herself, and stronger, she would have asked him to keep the door open. Her anger was as much directed toward herself as toward Mercer.

The door shut, Mercer walked toward her desk, stopping only a foot short of its edge, positioning himself so that he was looking down at her.

"You thought you were going to get away with it, didn't you, Judith? That cheap little trick. It wasn't even a trick. Sooner or later I'd have caught up with you. You know Farrell himself dismissed the case?"

She bit the inside of her lip, avoiding his gaze.

"No, I figured you'd find out, Aaron. I guess I just didn't care when you found out because Russell's not guilty, Whaley is. And I think you know it."

"Nothing to be surprised about, Judith. I do my job. That's all."

Judith stood and walked around the corner of her desk, toward him. "And since when does your job include prosecuting innocent people?"

"Innocence is for the jury to decide, not me. All I do is put the case on, that's all." He looked down at her hands. "You're hands are shaking Judith. I'm so sorry. I didn't mean to frighten you."

She hadn't noticed her hands were trembling until Mercer's comment. She was exactly where he wanted her to be, and she felt exactly the way he wanted her to feel. Small, vulnerable. This was how it was in this balance of power. He had it all. She had none. She was no better off than the secretaries he ordered into his office and proceeded to bully and harass. He regarded them all the same way. They were all women, and they were all there to do what he wanted. And that was principally to take it. Whatever it was he wanted them to take. It wasn't a macho thing, not a male thing. He was simply a man who needed to feel in control of others and required they knew he was in control. And Russell? He was in exactly the same boat. His innocence didn't matter unless and until Aaron Mercer said it did. And as for her, Judith? She was as powerless as the rest of them. Not only because Mercer wanted her in that position, but because she was allowing it. Forget the responsibility she had to Russell, or the secretaries in the office. She'd been allowing it to happen to her. For all of her experience as a prosecutor, her years in school, and her position of power within the office, she hadn't been able or willing to defend herself. But then, she never had been. Ever.

Judith held her hands up to her face, a slightly exaggerated movement. "Was I trembling? How uncharacteristic of me, Aaron." Judith stood and leaned on the side of her desk, toward the direction of Mercer. "It must have gotten colder in here when you closed the door."

Mercer took a half-step backward.

"Excuse me, I'm sorry, Aaron. No insult intended."

"None taken."

"Good, Aaron, good. I'd hate to damage our friendship. I know it means a lot to both of us." She didn't see his eyes narrow with her sarcasm. She walked out from behind her desk and stood next to him, looking up. He towered over her. Yet somehow at this moment the size differential didn't matter. She wasn't able to control her vocabulary, or the slow build from a quiet, gentle tone to a terse, clipped inflection.

"Have you ever watched anyone die, Aaron? I mean watched them die slowly, not fast, I mean over a long period of time, until there's nothing left of them, really. And there's nothing, nothing you can think of to help them. Or maybe tried to pick someone up off the floor after they've fallen. But you know they can't help you, can't even move their legs, and you know you can't lift them, and maybe they're going to have to stay there a while. And it's the middle of the night and you'd either have to wake a neighbor up to help or call the paramedics. Did you ever think someone you loved was dying right then, but you were wrong?" She took another step, even closer to him, and continued rapid-fire. "Ah, well, no, I'll bet you haven't. Well, you know, Aaron, *those* things are frightening. You? You're not frightening at all. In fact, nothing much *frightens* me anymore. So if I'm trembling, it's got to be the temperature. Now, where were we? Oh, yes, you're upset I filed a case against Whaley. Well, that's been taken care of, I assume to your satisfaction, so we really don't have a problem anymore, now, do we? It's Thomas Russell and his family who have the problem now. And you, Aaron, you have the problem now."

Her final comment made no impression on him. Indeed, she wasn't exactly certain what it was she meant. Mercer groped for words.

"I'm, I'm glad we see eye to eye on this now, Judith. And I'm assuming . . . well . . . I'll be going forward with the case without any further . . . any further. . . ."

" 'Interference,' Aaron, That's the word you're looking for."

"Exactly." If he'd been knocked momentarily off balance by her outburst, he'd recovered. "No further interference. I hate to see our friendship strained like this, Judith, over a case. These are the kinds of things that can come back to haunt you."

"Especially if your name's out for a judicial appointment, Aaron, right?"

Mercer was heading toward the door. His hand was on the doorknob when he turned toward her. "Right. In fact, Judith, I forgot to mention I just got an evaluation form for your possible appointment. It's on my desk."

Judith was incredulous. *He just doesn't give up. He had to let her know one last time who was in charge.*

To herself, barely audible, Judith responded, "Yours is on my desk, too, Aaron."

30

JUDITH FLIPPED THROUGH the pages of her trial schedule, looking for the status report on the Russell case. The preliminary hearing was three days away. After the dismissal of the Whaley case and her confrontation with Mercer, there was no stopping it from going forward. She tried her best to ignore it, and had almost succeeded for the morning, when the telephone rang. It was Larson.

"I suppose you're going to come down to see the prelim?" he asked.

"I don't think so," she shot back tersely.

"I've been able to get through all the reports and the interviews between Whaley and Pike Martin."

"Did you find anything interesting?"

"A little. I still intend to ask the judge to allow me to introduce evidence that Whaley committed the offense."

"That's going to be tough to do, Alan. Aaron will never let you get away with it."

"It's not up to him. I've got my ways, you know."

"Yeah. I know."

"Seriously, Judith, I want the judge to just hear the tapes. If I can get past that, I might have a fighting chance."

"Why are you telling me this, Alan? I can't do anything to help you. I'm officially out of the loop."

"I don't expect you to do anything. I just hope the tape's not too much of a surprise for Aaron."

"You can expect a battle."

"Can't wait. Maybe I'll be seeing you later."

"Oh, before you hang up, Alan, can I ask where you listened to the interview tape between Pike Martin and Whaley?"

"Evidence room. It's in the evidence room."

"Thanks, Alan. Sorry this didn't work out for the best."

"It's not over yet, Judith."

"Agreed."

Judith spent the morning working through the files on her desk. At noon she took a break and went down to the evidence room.

31

MARILYN RUSSELL RUBBED her hands together nervously, her eyes focused on the defense table where her husband sat, his head bent forward. He turned only once to look at her. The remainder of the time he sat, his head bent slightly forward, periodically exchanging thoughts with Alan Larson, who was seated next to him.

Larson had already carefully explained to his client and Marilyn Russell that the standard of proof to bind Russell over for a trial in Superior Court was a mere suspicion. The people at this stage did not have to prove guilt beyond a reasonable doubt. And the odds greatly favored the prosecution, even if the case against Russell was weak at this point. The judge assigned to the preliminary hearing was not known for making controversial decisions, especially in close cases. Since this was a crime against a minor, and a particularly heinous one at that, the court would not likely give much leeway to the defense. If it was a weak case, but enough to suspect Russell, the case would be set for trial.

Because of the lower standard of proof required at this hearing, Caryn wasn't in the courtroom. She'd been subpoenaed as a witness for the prosecution, but Mercer had asked, and received, the court's permission to call her at the end of his case. He first needed to get through the three police officers who arrived at the scene when the crime was reported, and the doctors who examined Caryn and determined a crime did exist. Mercer had also subpoenaed Marilyn Russell, but was determined not to call her, either, unless he felt it was absolutely necessary.

One by one the doctors were called. They testified in detail on the extent of Caryn's injuries and their medical opinions about the cause. Over Larson's objection, they were also permitted to testify to their experience in determining whether a child was not telling the truth and specifically whether Caryn Russell was telling the truth when she denied her father was the perpetrator of the crimes.

For his part, Larson was able to demonstrate there were lab tests which could have been done to determine the strength of the case against Russell. He methodically took the police officers through diagrams of the Russell house and the entrance point into the bedroom.

He asked them for their familiarity with the neighborhood and then came the question Mercer had been waiting for. Were any of the officers aware of other similar offenses within a three-mile radius of the Russell house?

Mercer leaped from his chair, spouting a

string of case authority on why the evidence of other crimes was irrelevant. Not to be outdone, Larson returned the attack, citing five out-of-state cases he claimed permitted such evidence at the discretion of the court. The result was an hour-long recess while the court read the cases. When the judge returned, the ruling was predictably against Larson. There would be no evidence introduced of similar crimes by others in the area of the Russell home.

At the end of the day, Mercer was struggling with the decision as to whether he would call Caryn Russell to the stand. She was still convinced her father had not molested her, and Mercer did not want to force that kind of evidence from her in a case which, objectively, had sufficient evidence to be bound over for trial without her.

The following morning it was Larson's turn to put on his defense, if any. He'd carefully explained to Russell that usually no defense was offered. There were several reasons for this. First, the chances of being sent on to Superior Court for trial were high. There was no reason to give away your evidence so the prosecutor could see it before trial. Second, unless the defendant had a strong defense, it was a waste of time. This time, however, Larson intended to put on a defense. Just what it was, he hadn't shared with his client.

The following morning, the judge called the case. Mercer was asked if there was anything further he wished to offer. There was nothing.

He obviously felt no need to have Caryn or her mother testify. And from the defense?

Larson rose slowly and turned to the bailiff.

"I'd like to call Arthur Whaley, please. Your Honor might want to call a recess. He's in the holding tank, Your Honor, and it may take some time to get him up here."

From the corner of his eye he could see Mercer bolt from his chair.

"I object, Your Honor, to the calling of this witness."

"On what ground?" the judge asked.

"On the ground his testimony is not relevant. Mr. Larson, true to form, is trying to get in the back door what he can't get in the front door."

The judge turned to Larson, expecting a response.

"Your Honor, I'd like to make an offer of proof, if I might."

"Go ahead, Mr. Larson."

"The witness, Mr. Whaley, has intimate knowledge of the offenses against Caryn Russell."

"That's not an offer of proof, Your Honor. I want to know just what he's going to testify to."

"Mr. Larson?"

"He's going to testify that he committed the offenses against Caryn Russell."

The courtroom erupted in noisy exchanges and exclamations from the attorneys and spectators.

"Order, please!" the judge cautioned, bringing the room to quiet control again before continuing. "Mr. Larson, did I hear correctly that this proposed witness wishes to tell this court that he committed the crimes for which Mr. Russell there has been charged?"

"That's correct, Your Honor."

"Mr. Mercer?"

"I most strongly object to this, Judge. This man who wants to confess to these crimes has just been convicted of a series of child molests here in San Diego. They are indeed similar to the Russell assaults. But he's been convicted and sentenced to prison for about the rest of his adult life. We can check the exact number of years—I'm certain Mr. Larson can pull that information for us. The point is, he has nothing to lose by admitting to this offense. I don't want to go into the details, but our office at one time tried to charge him with the crimes against Caryn Russell and ultimately we dismissed those charges as ill founded." Mercer turned to face Larson. "Mr. Larson knows better than this."

"Your Honor, if I can respond."

"Please, do so, Mr. Larson. This is a new one on me."

"Mr. Whaley admitted the offenses to me. If we cannot listen to him, then I would respectfully ask the court to listen to his taped admissions to the district attorney's own investigator, Mr. Pike Martin. Then you can decide for yourself if he ought to be called as a witness.

"Your Honor, I've listened to that tape. It was some time ago, but I have no objection to your screening it first before deciding whether to allow him to be called to the stand for live testimony. I believe it will support our position."

"Do you have any objection to my doing that, Mr. Mercer?"

"No . . . I don't think I do. But it doesn't change my argument one bit. Same thing applies for the tape. He has nothing to lose by taking the rap for the defendant here."

"How long until I can get the tape?"

"It's in the evidence room, Your Honor," Mercer offered.

"Well, let's take a brief recess and play it here in court, shall we? Let's have the clerk call it up from the evidence room. Court's in recess. Madame Clerk, let me know when you're ready to proceed."

With this, he rose and strode from the bench, leaving the attorneys and Thomas Russell waiting.

At the back of the courtroom, Judith Thornton held her breath.

Judith had been trying to stay as far back in the courtroom as possible. With the arrival, however, of the taped interview between Pike and Whaley, Judith moved to the front row.

It took several minutes to set up the tape recorder supplied by the district attorney's office. Judith watched as Mercer removed the tape from its brown envelope and took it to the judge's clerk to have it marked as an exhibit. The click of the recorder signaled the tape was in place and ready to be played for the judge, who appeared through the door behind the bench and climbed the three steps to her brown leather chair.

"We're ready to proceed, Counsel. For the record, we're going to be listening to a taped interview between one Arthur Whaley and detective Pike Martin. The tape's been marked?"

"It has been, Your Honor. Exhibit A for the defense," the court clerk responded.

"Then let's hear it, gentlemen."

The introduction of tapes was routine. But not this one. Judith clenched her fists as the tape began rolling and held her breath. The beginning of the tape was scratchy and not audible. Larson fast-forwarded. Judith listened as the high-pitched garble started and abruptly stopped. The tape was loud, filling the courtroom at once with the unmistakable voice of Aaron Mercer.

"You've got a boyfriend, haven't you? In fact I met him at the office holiday party."

"David?"

"David, right. Nice-looking young man.

*Bright, too. Let me ask you, Martha . . .
are those the kind of things you and
David do? (Silence) Oh, Martha . . ."*

It took Mercer several minutes to recognize the conversation on the tape as that between himself and Martha Salinger in the privacy of his office. At the precise moment of recognition, he leaped forward and slapped the stop button, leaving the court, the spectators, and Alan Larson, bewildered.

"Mr. Mercer . . . what was that? It's certainly not an interview between Mr. Russell and Detective Martin."

"It's not . . . it's really . . . well, it's supposed to be a test tape . . . a test of . . . of—"

"It's a test tape, Your Honor, of the transcript from one of Mr. Mercer's cases."

There was a rustle throughout the courtroom as heads turned to the spectator section and Judith Thornton stepped into the well of the courtroom.

"It's fortunate I was here, Aaron. That tape's the one your secretary gave me to file, and I'm afraid it somehow got mislabeled. I'll take it back to its correct file. The sexual harassment case you've been working so hard on. It's really one of a series of them." She stepped toward the tape recorder, pushed the eject button, and removed the tape. Then she looked up at the judge. "Is that okay, Your Honor?"

Mercer stumbled backward, too stunned and confused to respond.

"I suppose so, Mrs. Thornton. I assume, Mr. Mercer, that you can get the correct tape to us this afternoon?"

His voice was a whisper. "Ah . . . ah, I, yes, certainly, Your Honor. You'll have it this afternoon."

"One-thirty, then, Counsel. Court's in recess."

When the bailiff removed Russell from the courtroom, Judith turned to Mercer.

"I'd suggest, Aaron, that you listen to the tape of that interview. It's on your desk. Then maybe you can take a look at the files on Whaley's offenses. I think you need to reconsider the charges in this case."

Judith turned and walked toward the doors of the courtroom.

"Judith! Wait."

Alan Larson put his hand on Judith's shoulder, stopping her as she was about to step into the hallway.

"What was that?"

"What was what?"

"That." He pointed toward the cassette tape in her hand.

"Don't ask."

"I have to, because whatever it was, it was brilliant."

"In the parlance of the soccer field, let's just say it was the perfect slide tackle."

"Slide-what?"

"It's where the guy's running down the field with the ball, heading for the goal, and you're the defender, see, and you have to run like hell to catch him. And when you do, you slide, right into his feet, and kick the ball free. It's legal if you hit the ball. If you clip the guy, you've got yourself a foul. That one was close, Alan."

"That isn't a transcript on the tape, is it?"

Judith smiled and shrugged.

"I'll be damned. I didn't think you had it in you."

"Neither did I, Mr. Larson. Neither did I. I'll see you at one-thirty."

She left Larson standing by the courtroom doors, watching her walk toward the escalator to her office.

"Come in, Aaron. I expected you'd be here a lot sooner."

Mercer stepped into her office and closed the door behind him.

"I'd like the tape back."

"Now, which tape is that?"

"You know damned well which tape I mean. The tape of my conversation with Martha Salinger. The one played in court today. And if you don't mind, I'd like to know how you got it."

"To your first request, I've got it in a safe place. Don't worry. To your second request, it's irrelevant where I got it."

"Are you trying to blackmail me, Judith? Because if you are . . ."

"I'm not blackmailing you, Aaron. I'm requesting you carefully consider the defendant in that courtroom. I'm requesting you think about his future as well as your own. Balance the equities. Yours and his."

"What if you're wrong, Judith? What if Whaley didn't do it?"

"I'm not wrong."

"Your Honor, the People have a motion to make."

"Go ahead, Mr. Mercer."

Alan Larson caught his breath and turned to his client. "My God," he whispered.

"What's happening, Alan?" Russell whispered, a puzzled look on his face.

"Just listen. I don't believe this," Larson said, more to himself than to Russell.

"Your Honor, the People move to dismiss the charges against Thomas Russell."

A piercing scream shattered the calm proceeding as Marilyn Russell held her hands to her face and began sobbing uncontrollably.

"Mr. Larson, I assume your client has no objection?" the judge asked.

"No. No objection at all."

"Then in the interest of justice, the charges against Thomas Russell are hereby dismissed. The defendant is to be released forthwith."

As soon as the judge left the courtroom, Mercer shoved his notes and papers into his file folder. He didn't say a word to Larson, but left quickly for his office without noticing Judith Thornton, sitting in the last row, to the right, in the furthest seat from the doors. But her presence did not escape Larson. As Russell's wife ran through the wooden rail gate separating her from her husband, Larson turned to Judith and smiled.

Epilogue

JUDITH COULD SEE the rain coming in over the ocean; above it lay deep gray clouds with fingers extending downward to the water. The soccer tournament would go on, however, despite a downpour. She'd agreed to help field marshal the all-day event. For her, it was a respite, standing in the rain with an umbrella and a cup of hot coffee. It didn't much matter to her if she got wet.

Elizabeth's team was about to start playing at the west end of the field, but she'd been assigned to the east end, where the boys' games were being played. She recognized the home team.

"What's the score?" Judith asked the woman standing next to her, obviously a parent of one of the boys.

"Zero–zero. But we'll win. See their center midfield? It won't hold up in the second half."

"It looks strong . . ."

"Nah. Wait. See their kid in the middle? Their midfielder?"

"Yeah . . ."

"My Jason'll bump him; he'll go down and won't get up."

The two women stared out over the field, and true to her prediction, within minutes the center midfielder found himself with the ball, pursued by the woman's son.

"Get him, Jason!" the woman shrieked over the field, her voice rising. Jason was bigger, and also taller by several inches. By all rights, he should have stolen control of the ball. But when they collided, it was the smaller midfielder who stayed on his feet.

The parents lining the field yelled, to the referee, to the opposing coach, to no one in particular. "What happened?" "No whistle?" "That's a yellow card!"

But Judith saw the play, saw the midfielder's hands tuck under Jason's shirt. She saw the pull. Not a hard one, just enough to throw his opponent off balance.

A minute or two later the midfielder trotted off the field and a substitute took his place. Judith watched as the boy's coach walked over to him and laying his arm across the boy's shoulder, whispered, "Well done."

Acknowledgments

For those of us who follow closely the game
of soccer, there may be an added level to this
book as the characters, particularly Judith, maneuver on their own playing fields. The author
would like to thank the coaching staff of the
Nomads Soccer Club in La Jolla, in particular
its coaching director, Derek Armstrong; Tony
Parker; and Manny Diaz. Over the course of
two years, they provided a field from which
to observe this nationally recognized organization train young men and women, including
my son Peter, in a sport which demands not
only extraordinary physical stamina and skill
but intelligence as well.

And, as always, my thanks and love to Michael for his support and help when the field
seems obscured.